RUINED LIES

THE BILLIONAIRES OF CREST STRATEGIES
BOOK 1

ELORA RAE

ALSO BY ELORA RAE

The Billionaires Of Crest Strategies

Ruined Lies

Tattered Secrets

Salvaged Vows

Coded Truths

Wrecked Fates

To everyone who's ever said "yes sir" to a book.

TRIGGER/CONTENT WARNING

Hey gorgeous (likely unhinged) readers!

This novella is a dark billionaire romance.

Before you dive into Carson and Kinsley's deliciously twisted love story, let's chat about what you're getting into because we all know that in this genre, content warnings are how we choose books...

Inside this book, you'll find:
- **Psychological manipulation and stalking**: Our MMC has been playing a very long, very calculated surveillance game
- **Mentions of suicide and mental health struggles**: A character's past includes depression and suicide (handled with care, but present in the backstory)
- **Violence and blood**: Including kidnapping, gun violence, and threats that get very real in the third act
- **Power imbalances and emotional control**: Lines between real and fake get very, very blurry
- **Excessive swearing and profanity**: Self explanatory

• **Spicy, high-heat sex scenes**: With a possessive billionaire who has zero chill and doesn't always play fair

Other content warnings: Possibility of SA (does not actually happen, but it is suggested), mild power play during sex, choking and slapping during sex, public sexual activities, torture with a cattle prod, attempted murder, actual murder which of course means death on page.

I did say it was dark...

The good news? This is consensual dark billionaire romance. We LOVE clear consent here.

If any of these themes are upsetting or not your thing, please take care while reading, or maybe skip this one. There are lots of amazing books out there, so find the ones that bring you joy, not stress.

But if you're here for a twisted, sexy, high-stakes rollercoaster where you'll naturally root for the handsome stalker...

Welcome to the *Billionaires of Crest Strategies*.

You've been warned.

Happy reading!

-Elora

CHAPTER ONE

KINSLEY

KINSLEY DELETED THE APOLOGY POST FOR THE SIXTH TIME and wanted to throw her phone through the penthouse window.

The cursor mocked her, blinking in the empty text box while her follower count hemorrhaged in real time. 2.1 million. Refresh. 2.08 million. Refresh. 2.05 million. Each lost follower was a small death, validation bleeding out through her fingertips while she sat paralyzed on her bathroom floor.

Thirty-seven seconds. That's all it had taken to destroy years of carefully curated perfection.

Her reflection stared back from the Hollywood vanity mirror—hollow-eyed, breakouts scattered across her usually flawless brown skin, dark curls matted against her skull. The girl who'd built an empire on being beautiful, relatable, palatable looked like she'd crawled out of a grave.

Maybe she had.

The hot mic incident played on loop in her head: *"Let's be honest, they're too stupid to know I'm selling them garbage half the time. As long as I smile pretty and tell them it changed my life, they'll buy anything."*

She'd meant every word. That was the problem.

Kinsley's phone erupted with notifications. A fresh wave of digital violence she couldn't stop consuming. The comments section of her last post had become a public execution.

Finally, showing your true colors, you fake btch*

Hope you lose everything

Your parents must be so ashamed

Delete your account and disappear

The cruelest part? They were right. She had been fake, selling them dreams wrapped in designer packaging while secretly despising their eagerness to believe. She'd perfected the art of being just enough—pretty enough, relatable enough, unthreatening enough—to make millions off their insecurities.

And now they were returning the favor.

Her phone rang. Mom's contact photo smiled back at her; a family portrait from Christmas where they'd all pretended to be closer than they were.

"Kinsley." Her mother's voice carried a familiar note of barely controlled disappointment. "The neighbors are asking questions."

"I didn't mean for anyone to hear—"

"But you said it. You meant it. Do you have any idea how this reflects on our family? Your father's law practice, my reputation at the club? We raised you better than this."

Kinsley's throat closed. Better than what? Better than telling the truth? "I was having a bad day—"

"Fix this. Whatever it takes. And don't call until you do."

The line went dead.

Kinsley stared at the phone, her mother's conditional love ringing in her ears. She'd spent twenty-five years trying to be the daughter they wanted. Polite, successful, never too loud or too much. Even her career had been an extension of that performance, turning herself into a product designed for mass consumption.

Being too much equals being alone.

The lesson had been beaten into her since childhood, reinforced by every comment that called her "angry" when she expressed opinions, every brand deal that required her to soften her edges until she'd forgotten she had any.

But now the performance had cracked, and everyone could see the machinery underneath.

Her phone chimed with an email notification. Chanel, demanding their products back. Another chime. Dior. Gucci. All the brands that had once courted her were now fleeing like rats from a sinking ship.

Eighteen thousand in past-due rent. Her management had dropped her. Her credit cards were maxed.

She was twenty-five years old and she'd just discovered that everything she'd built her identity on was as fake as they said she was.

The bottle of sleeping pills rattled in her shaking hands. Ambien. Prescribed for stress-induced insomnia back when her biggest worry was maintaining her posting schedule. The irony wasn't lost on her. She'd been having trouble sleeping because she was so busy performing happiness, and now she might never wake up because the performance had finally cracked.

Just a few. Just enough to make it stop.

Her thumb traced the prescription label while her phone buzzed endlessly beside her. More notifications. More hate. More people celebrating her downfall with the same enthusiasm they'd once brought to her content.

She unscrewed the cap.

The pills scattered across the marble like confetti at the worst party of her life. Twenty-three left. Probably enough. Definitely enough if she chased them with the bottle of wine she'd been nursing since this morning.

This wasn't supposed to happen to her. She'd been strategic, calculated, careful. She'd studied every successful influencer, analyzed every algorithm change, optimized every post for maximum engagement. She'd turned herself into a machine designed to generate likability.

Kinsley stared at nothing for several minutes. It would be easier if all the noise stopped. She grabbed a handful of the pills and brought them to her mouth.

Her phone buzzed with a different sound. A DM notification. Probably another death threat or creative suggestion about what she should do with her platform. She almost ignored it.

The profile had no picture.

> I can help you fix this. I know what they did to you isn't fair. -C

Kinsley stared at the message, her pulse quickening. It could be a reporter. A scammer. Another person looking to profit from her misery.

But it was the first message in three days that didn't tell her she deserved to burn.

She typed back.

> Who is this?

The response came immediately.

> Someone who understands what it's like to be destroyed by a single moment. Someone who's helped others rebuild from worse. Are you ready to do whatever it takes to get your life back?

Whatever it takes. The phrase should have been a warning. Instead, it seemed like salvation.

Kinsley looked at the pills scattered around her, then at the message promising redemption. She thought about the girl she'd been before the followers and the money. She'd been loud, opinionated, unafraid to take up space. That girl had been steamrolled by parents who valued politeness over authenticity, by an industry that rewarded palatability over personality.

Maybe it was time to stop being palatable.

Maybe it was time to be too much.

She swept the pills back into the bottle with one hand and typed with the other.

> Yes. I'll do anything.

Good. Meet me tomorrow night. The Meridian
Hotel, charity gala for the Manhattan Mental
Health Foundation. Wear red. I'll find you.

The conversation ended, leaving her staring at the screen with something she hadn't felt in days: possibility.

Not hope.

That felt too dangerous. But the chance that this wasn't the end of her story.

She didn't know who C was or how they planned to save her. But for the first time since the hot mic incident, she felt something other than the crushing weight of public shame.

Something darker stirred. Something that whispered that maybe she didn't want to disappear quietly. Maybe she wanted to fight back. Maybe the girl who'd learned to make herself small was ready to remember what it felt like to be too much.

The pills could wait.

Someone thought she was worth saving.

Time to find out if they were right.

CHAPTER TWO

CARSON

CARSON CREST HAD BEEN WATCHING KINSLEY ELLIS self-destruct for hours, and he was getting hard from it.

Not from her pain. He wasn't completely without a conscience. But from the control. The precision. Four and a half years of meticulous planning turned into thirty-seven seconds that started the downfall. The best part was she'd done it herself by her own words. She'd destroyed everything she'd built. Every follower lost, every sponsor fleeing, every piece of her perfect life crumbling exactly as he'd orchestrated.

But Kinsley had pulled the trigger.

She'd called her followers stupid. He'd simply ensured the entire world heard it.

His corner office on the forty-second floor stood over Manhattan with large ceiling to floor windows, but Carson's attention fixed on the wall of monitors tracking his obsession. Six screens displayed Kinsley's digital suicide in real time: follower counts disappearing, brand partnerships evaporating, her credit score nosediving as payments bounced. The surveillance feed from her building showed she hadn't left her penthouse since the scandal broke.

Perfect. Let her marinate in consequences while he savored every moment of her fall.

Carson adjusted his platinum cufflinks and pulled up the thermal imaging from her apartment. The red outline of her body moved through the rooms like a caged animal. She was pacing again. The same pattern she'd repeated every few hours since Tuesday. Kitchen to living room to bathroom, pause at the mirror, back to the couch where she'd check her phone and start the cycle again.

He knew her routines better than she did. What time she typically went to bed (2 AM), what she ate when stressed (nothing, just energy drinks), how long her breakdowns lasted (approximately eighteen minutes before she forced herself to function again). Four and a half years of surveillance had made him fluent in the language of Kinsley Ellis.

The silver picture frame on his desk caught the afternoon light. Emma's graduation photo, her smile bright with trust that had cost her everything. Four and a half years dead because an influencer thought someone else's breakdown was content worth capturing.

"She'll pay, Em," Carson murmured to the photograph, his fingers tracing his dead fiancée's face through the glass. The same promise he'd made at her funeral while Kinsley's video played on repeat across every social platform.

His jaw clenched as the familiar rage coursed through him. Emma had deserved better than the world that killed her. Better than a fiancé who'd failed to protect her. Better than dying because some narcissistic influencer had prioritized content over compassion.

Carson had built Crest Strategies into the most appreciated and feared reputation management firm in New York by understanding exactly how to build up those he deemed worthy, and to destroy people like Kinsley Ellis. Entitled influencers who profited from others' suffering, who treated real human pain like entertainment, who smiled and waved their way to millions while leaving devastation in their wake.

Seventeen secret successful takedowns, both individuals and businesses, in only a few years.

But those targets hadn't been responsible for Emma's death.

Those targets hadn't consumed his thoughts for four and a half years.

Those targets hadn't made him dream about their destruction in ways that felt increasingly less like justice and more like obsession.

Those targets hadn't been personal. None had been for Emma.

The surveillance feed showed Kinsley collapse onto her bathroom floor, and Carson's pulse quickened. She looked smaller than she had three days ago, more fragile. The designer clothes hung loose on her shrinking frame. Her famous curls—the ones that had launched a thousand hair care partnerships—were matted and greasy.

He leaned forward in his chair, his expensive suit suddenly feeling too tight. There was something mesmerizing about watching her break apart piece by piece, knowing he held every thread of her unraveling. She had no idea he existed, no clue that her destruction had an architect.

The monitor showed her reaching for something. A prescription bottle. Carson's blood turned to ice as pills scattered across her marble floor like deadly confetti.

"No." The word escaped him before he could stop it, his hand pressed flat against the screen. Not like this. Not quick and easy and private. She needed to understand what she'd cost him first. She needed to suffer the way Emma had suffered. Publicly, thoroughly, with the whole world watching and mocking.

Carson forced himself to breathe, to regain control. His reaction had nothing to do with concern for Kinsley's wellbeing. He'd simply invested too much time and energy in her destruction to let her take the easy way out. All of his planning deserved a more satisfying conclusion.

He pulled up the video that had started everything. The charity gala where Emma had suffered her breakdown while Kinsley filmed herself across the room. The footage showed Kinsley laughing with friends, completely oblivious to Emma's distress just meters away. She'd been too busy creating content to notice real human suffering unfolding beside her.

But that wasn't the worst part. The worst part came later, when Kinsley posted the video with the caption: "Amazing night supporting mental health awareness! Sometimes the most authentic moments happen when you're just being yourself! #RealTalk #Authentic #MentalHealthMatters"

She'd used Emma's breakdown as a backdrop for her own brand messaging. Mental health hashtags to boost engagement while a woman died from the very thing Kinsley was commodifying.

Carson's hands clenched into fists as he relived that night. Emma locked in their bathroom for hours afterward, reading every cruel comment about her "public meltdown." The internet had turned her worst moment into entertainment, dissecting her pain with the detached cruelty of strangers who saw her as content rather than human.

"Look at the crazy girl in the background," one comment had read.

"Main character energy vs. side character reality," said another.

Emma had screenshotted every single one.

A week later, she was dead.

Carson pulled out his laptop and began crafting the message that would change everything. On the surveillance feed, Kinsley stared at the scattered pills, her shoulders shaking. Perfect timing.

> I can help you fix this. I know what they did to you isn't fair. -C

He hovered over send, watching her reach for the bottle again. The moment had to be precise. He had to catch her at the exact second of maximum desperation.

His phone rang. Carson glanced at the caller ID and grimaced. Paisley only called when she needed something or wanted to lecture him about his life choices.

"Carson?" His sister's voice carried through the phone speaker. "I'm calling about the Mental Health Foundation board meeting next week. I know you hate these things, but we need your vote on the new funding initiative."

"Which initiative?" Carson kept his eyes on the monitor, watching Kinsley's hands tremble as she unscrewed the pill bottle cap.

"The digital wellness program. Online harassment support, suicide prevention outreach, that sort of thing. It's become such a huge problem. Just this week one of my friends got completely destroyed online for some stupid comment. Poor Kinsley's been hiding in her apartment for days."

Carson's finger froze over the send button. "Kinsley?"

"Kinsley Ellis. You probably don't know her. She's an influencer. But she's actually really sweet when she's not performing for cameras. I'm worried about her."

"Mm." Carson made his voice sound appropriately disinterested while his pulse quickened. Paisley was friends with his target. The universe had just handed him a perfect entry point. "These influencer scandals happen constantly."

"I know, but this feels different. More vicious. Like someone's orchestrating it, you know?"

"That *is* unfortunate. Why don't you invite her to the gala. Maybe I could speak to her. I am in the business of reputations after all."

"Would you do that?"

Carson tilted his head, smirking at the monitors. "I think I can make time for it if you'll make the introduction."

"That would be wonderful! Thank you, Cars." Paisley's smile came through the phone purely by the joy in her voice.

He wrinkled his nose. Paisley was the last person he'd want to get hurt, and he'd have to make sure he kept her out of his plan.

"Of course, Pai."

"Sweet," she said, and by the sound coming from her phone, he knew she'd started chewing on her thumbnail because her words came out muffled. "Anyway, can I count on your vote for the funding?"

"Yes. Send me the details."

Kinsley moved again on screen, collecting the pills. Carson's heart rate sped up.

"I have a meeting. Love you," he said. Carson ended the call and immediately hit send on the message. On screen, Kinsley's phone buzzed just as she raised a handful of pills to her lips.

He watched her read his words, saw her shoulders straighten slightly. She typed back quickly, desperately.

Who is this?

Carson prepared his response and sent it, grinning when she replied exactly as he'd hoped.

Yes. I'll do anything.

Good. We'll talk soon. Trust me, Kinsley. You're not as alone as you think.

Carson leaned back in his chair, satisfaction coursing through him. Phase One complete. Kinsley Ellis was now primed for salvation— salvation that would come in the form of her own destruction.

On the surveillance feed, she swept the pills back into their bottle and set her phone down with something approaching hope on her face. She had no idea she'd just sealed her fate.

He touched Emma's photograph one last time. At the very same venue where his fiancée had died, he would meet the woman responsible face to face. "Soon, Em. She'll know what it feels like to lose everything because of the world she helped create."

The irony would be lost on Kinsley, but Carson would remember every detail of that night as he began the final phase of her destruction.

Carson had spent years becoming very good at reading people's breaking points. He'd learned patience from necessity, precision from practice, and cruelty from grief. Kinsley Ellis represented everything wrong with the culture that had killed Emma. Everything wrong. The performative empathy, the commodified suffering, the complete disconnect between online persona and human decency.

She would pay for all of it.

And thanks to Paisley's misguided friendship, Carson now had the perfect way in.

Outside his windows, Manhattan glittered with another night's possibilities. Another perfectly calculated move in the game he'd been playing since Emma died.

And Carson never lost.

Carson's muscles tensed at the sharp knock on his office door. Three precise raps. Benedict's signature. He swept his finger across the tablet control panel, instantly blacking out the wall of monitors displaying Kinsley's apartment. The digital command center transformed into an innocuous display of market projections and client analytics within seconds.

"Come in," he called.

Benedict Astor pushed the door open, his lean frame impeccably dressed in a tailored navy suit that probably cost more than most people's monthly rent. He scanned the room. Carson smiled and welcomed him farther in.

"Ben. What has you joining me this lovely afternoon?"

"What's with the good mood?" It was this, Benedict's hyperawareness, that made him Crest Strategies' most valuable asset. And the most dangerous, if anyone knew what they were looking for.

"The sun is out for the first time in weeks," Carson said, gesturing to the panoramic view. "It's got me smiling."

"It's creepy."

"What do you want, Benny?"

"Well for one, I'd like you to stop looking at me like a serial killer looks at his next victim." He pointed to his own mouth, and Carson rolled his eyes but lessened the wide smile he'd been wearing. "Good. And two, the others are waiting in the conference room." Benedict's gaze lingered briefly on Carson's desk where Emma's photo sat. "Quarterly projections and strategy. Tanner's getting impatient."

"When isn't he?" Carson closed the laptop and pocketed his phone. "Tell me Penn isn't trying to hack the building's climate control again."

"He claims the temperature is 'optimized for mediocrity.' His words, not mine." A ghost of a smile crossed Benedict's face. "James brought the legal briefs for the Richardson acquisition."

Carson nodded, gathering his tablet and straightening his tie. Benedict remained in the doorway, his posture relaxed but his eyes missing nothing. They'd been friends since school, partners through hours of endless work, and now the architects of the most appreciated and feared reputation management firm in the country. Benedict knew all of Carson's tells.

Well, almost all of them.

"You seem... focused today," Benedict observed, his tone casual in a way that wasn't casual at all. "New potential project?"

Carson met his gaze. "Just tying up loose ends on the Ashford case."

"The Ashford case we closed three years ago?"

"There were complications."

Benedict's eyebrow arched, but he didn't push further. It was their unspoken agreement. Respect each other's work until the secrets being kept threatened the company. They'd all built Crest Strategies on the foundation of their particular talents: Carson's strategic brilliance, Benedict's surveillance expertise, Penn's digital manipulation, James's legal maneuvering, and Tanner's ability to make problems disappear permanently.

Each of them had their own projects. Their own ghosts.

Together, Crest Strategies became something that existed in the spaces between legal and illegal, helping some clients while secretly and systematically destroying others. The business world's most feared and most necessary evil.

"Tanner brought scotch," Benedict said finally, stepping back from the doorway. "The good kind, not the pretentious kind."

"There's a difference?"

"According to him, one costs five figures and the other tastes like 'actual fucking Scotland.'"

Carson laughed despite himself. He tucked his tablet and files under his arm, making sure the surveillance feeds were completely disconnected from his devices.

As they walked down the hallway toward the conference room, voices echoed, getting louder the closer they got. Penn and James's argument about cryptocurrency regulations and Tanner's deep voice cutting through with his typical colorful profanity. His team of brilliant, powerful, dangerous men who had built an empire on understanding how information shaped reality.

He saw them all as brothers, which likely got on his only real sibling's nerves. But if anyone could handle them, it was Paisley. Hell, she'd known Benedict almost as long as he had. She would've been fine with five older brothers, though he was sure she was grateful she only had one to contend with.

All of the Crest Strategies men knew about Emma.

Had seen Carson at his lowest.

None of them, though, knew about Kinsley. About the revenge plot he'd been crafting for years. And he intended to keep it that way.

His phone vibrated in his pocket just as they reached the conference room door. Carson paused, pulling it out to check the notification.

A DM. It was the secure line he'd used to contact Kinsley.

Two words glowed on the screen.

Thank you.

Carson's lips curved into a smile that would have chilled anyone who truly knew what it meant. Benedict glanced back, catching the expression before Carson could mask it.

"Good news?" Benedict asked.

Carson slipped the phone back into his pocket, the satisfaction still humming through his veins. "Just someone expressing their gratitude for my... intervention."

"Must be quite the intervention."

"Oh, it will be."

CHAPTER THREE

KINSLEY

Kinsley stared at her reflection in the Meridian Hotel's gold-framed mirror and wondered if she was about to make a deal with the devil.

The red dress embraced her curves like liquid fire. She'd spent the last of her available cash on hair and makeup, determined to look like someone worth saving rather than someone beyond redemption.

A day ago, she'd been ready to swallow a bottle of pills. Now she was about to walk into a room full of Manhattan's elite, hunting for a stranger who claimed he could resurrect her career from its digital grave.

She didn't miss the irony. She was performing again, just for an audience of one.

The Manhattan Mental Health Foundation gala sparkled around her. She'd attended the same charity event four years ago, when her world had been perfect and her biggest worry was which designer wanted to dress her next. Now she moved through the crowd like a ghost haunting her former life.

Conversations stuttered when people recognized her. Eyes tracked her movement with the fascination of watching a car accident in slow motion. The same faces who'd celebrated her success last month now watched her like she might contaminate them through proximity.

All except one.

Across the ballroom, a man in a charcoal suit stood still near the bar, his attention focused entirely on her. Even from a distance, she could feel the weight of his gaze as it traveled up and down her figure. Everything about him screamed power. From the precise way he held his whiskey glass to the calculating intensity in his steel-gray eyes.

Her pulse quickened.

Why was he staring at her and why did he look so familiar?

She answered the question by reminding herself that half the people there were rich and famous. Likely, she'd seen his very handsome face online or on television or something.

"Kinsley?" Paisley Crest appeared at her elbow, genuine concern etched across her freckled face. "I wasn't sure you'd come. How are you surviving?" Paisley was one of the few people who hadn't blocked her number when the scandal broke.

Barely. "I'm managing. Thanks for the invitation."

"Of course. You know you're always—" Paisley stopped mid-sentence, following Kinsley's gaze to the bar. "Oh. You've spotted my brother. I was actually planning to introduce you two."

"Your brother?"

"Carson Crest. The tall one who looks like he could dismantle someone's entire existence with a single phone call." Paisley's voice carried fond exasperation. "He probably could, actually. Reputation management is his specialty. He's been staring at you since you walked in. I think he sees you as a potential client and is planning to offer you Crest Strategies' services. He has a weakness for helping people rebuild from impossible situations."

Kinsley's breath caught. Carson Crest.

She knew vaguely about Crest Strategies. Her ex-manager had told her that it was the firm that could make scandals disappear or destroy careers.

If *C* was Carson Crest, then he wasn't just offering to help her.

He was offering to own her.

"He would help? What…What kind of help?" Kinsley asked carefully, her gaze never leaving Carson's.

"Reputation management. Crisis response. He's rebuilt careers from worse wreckage than yours." Paisley's smile turned mischievous. "Plus he's single, brilliant, and looks at you like he wants to devour you whole. Could be exactly what you need." She winced. "As long as you tell me absolutely no details." Paisley wrinkled her freckled nose. "I have no desire to hear about my brother's sexual exploits."

"You'd be *lucky* to hear about my exploits," Carson said, a mischievous grin on his lips when his sister jumped. He'd managed to sneak up behind Paisley, holding a rather large finger up to his lips to keep Kinsley from saying anything.

"Damn it, Cars!" Paisley pinched her lips together and glared at her brother. "Jerk."

"Bitch."

Paisley looked about ready to strangle her brother, but Kinsley stepped in before she got the chance.

"Carson? I'm Kinsley Ellis. I'm friends with your sister. I—" Every word she'd been about to say disappeared when Carson took her offered hand with his free one and brought it up to his lips. He placed a light kiss over the knuckles.

"Kinsley Ellis." Carson's tone took on a deeper note, and it caused Kinsley's stomach to tighten. The smirk on his lips was nothing short of rakish. "You look lovely tonight."

"Thank you." She wasn't sure what else to say as Carson released her hand and it fell back to her side. "You work at that reputation company?"

He chuckled and downed the rest of his glass, placing it on a server's tray as they passed by. "Pai, were you gossiping about me again?"

Paisley rolled her eyes. "I hate you."

Carson winked at her. "Yes, Ms. Ellis, I'm the CEO of Crest Strategies. I hear you might be in need of a little reputation clean up. Is that correct?"

Kinsley glanced at Paisley, who was rolling her eyes. "Um, yes."

"I should let you two talk," Paisley said, glancing between them. "I need to check on the auction items. Carson, be nice to her."

Carson's smile was sharp enough to cut. "I'm always nice to beautiful women in distress."

As Paisley disappeared into the crowd, Carson stepped closer. Not inappropriately close, but near enough that Kinsley caught the warmth radiating from his body, near enough to see how his pupils dilated when he looked at her.

"You came," he said simply. Kinsley felt pinned like a butterfly to a board as Carson's gaze traveled over her red dress with an intensity that made her skin feel hypersensitive.

"You're C? I mean, that would make sense considering your name." Kinsley bit her bottom lip.

"And my job." His gaze tracked her movement, and he stared at her lips as he responded.

"Right."

"I'm glad you took the invitation." He drew his attention back to her eyes.

"Considering the fact that my life has gone to hell in a designer hand basket, I didn't really have a choice."

"Everyone has choices, Ms. Ellis. The question is whether they're brave enough to make the hard ones." His gaze drifted over her face again. "You look... recovered."

"Appearances can be deceiving."

"They certainly can. Shall we find somewhere more private? I imagine you have questions."

He didn't wait for her response, his hand settling on the small of her back to guide her toward a secluded alcove. The touch was brief, professional, but it burned through the thin fabric of her dress.

Carson positioned himself so he could see the entire room while keeping her partially hidden from view.

"Why would you help me?" Kinsley asked, searching Carson's face for any hint of deception. "I've been turned away by every PR firm in the city. I'm toxic."

"I specialize in toxic." His voice carried an edge that made her wonder if there was more to his offer than professional interest. "What happened to you wasn't entirely fair."

Kinsley's eyebrows shot up. "Most people think I got exactly what I deserved."

"Most people are sheep following whatever narrative is fed to them." Carson leaned closer, his cologne wrapping around her senses.

"So this isn't a game to you, right?" Desperation leaked into her voice despite her best efforts. "Because I can't afford games right now."

"Games?" Carson stepped closer, close enough that she had to tilt her head back to maintain eye contact. "Ms. Ellis, what's happening to you isn't a game. I suspect it's systematic destruction. I would wager quite a bit of money that someone is orchestrating your downfall."

Kinsley could've sworn she stopped breathing. "What do you mean?"

"Your scandal didn't just go viral organically. It seems someone amplified it. Bot networks, paid trolls, strategic media placements. This level of coordinated attack requires resources and expertise. I've seen it before. Hell, I've orchestrated it before."

Kinsley's knees went weak. "Why would someone do that to me, though?"

Carson's eyes glittered. "Perhaps you have enemies you're not aware of. Perhaps someone sees you as a threat." He took another glass of amber liquid from a server and sipped before continuing. "Perhaps you simply made someone very angry."

"But you can fix it?" The question came out smaller than she intended.

"I can do better than fix it." His voice dropped to an intimate whisper. "I can make you untouchable."

"What would that cost me?"

Carson tilted his head, studying her with the intensity of a scientist examining a specimen. "An interesting question. Most people ask what I want, not what it will cost them."

"Is there a difference?"

"Yes." He reached into his jacket and pulled out a sleek tablet. "But in your case, I think we can come to a mutually beneficial arrangement."

The tablet materialized like he'd been planning this moment.

"I've taken the liberty of drafting a preliminary agreement. It's something all my clients sign first," Carson continued, his fingers brushing hers as he handed her the device. "It outlines a partnership that could solve both our problems."

Kinsley stared at the screen, her hands trembling. "What kind of partnership?"

"The kind where you get your life back, and I get positive publicity for my business. Think of it as strategic rehabilitation through association."

The contract filled the screen, dense legal language that made her head spin. But certain phrases jumped out: *complete social media access, financial oversight, emergency decision-making authority, exclusive representation.*

"This is very comprehensive," she managed.

"I believe in thoroughness." Carson moved behind her, close enough that his breath lifted the baby hairs on her neck. "I'm proposing a partnership," he said, his voice low and hypnotic. "Crest Strategies will handle your complete image rehabilitation. We'll expose the people who destroyed you, eliminate future threats, and rebuild your reputation from the ground up."

"In exchange for what?"

"Your complete trust. Your absolute cooperation with our strategies. Your willingness to let us guide every aspect of your public recovery." Carson's hand settled on her waist, the touch light but possessive. "And perhaps something more."

"More?" She turned to face him, stepping back when she realized how close he was.

"The media loves a redemption story, especially when it involves romance. You'd be seen with someone respectable, someone untouchable. The narrative practically writes itself. The disgraced influencer saved by the man who believes in second chances."

"Who?"

"Me."

Heat flooded her system. Somehow, the idea of belonging to someone this powerful, this controlled, felt like sanctuary after days of drowning.

"You're talking about a fake dating relationship?"

"I'm talking about a strategic partnership that serves both our interests." Carson's thumb traced along her jawline. "Though who's to say what's real and what's performance when the chemistry is this undeniable?"

"What would you need from me?" she asked, her voice barely above a whisper.

"Everything." The word was soft, absolute. "Your trust, your compliance, your complete surrender to my guidance. I'd manage every aspect of your public image until we've rebuilt your reputation from ashes."

Complete surrender. The phrase should have terrified her.

It felt like relief.

"This gives you enormous control over my life."

"Control is what's been missing from your situation, Ms. Ellis. Someone needs to take the wheel before you crash completely." Carson's eyes blazed. "The question is whether you trust me to drive."

Kinsley looked around the ballroom at the faces that had turned away from her, at the life she'd lost, at the future that looked increasingly impossible to reclaim on her own. Carson was right. She'd been spiraling for days, making reactive decisions, letting her emotions drive her choices. She needed someone stronger, someone smarter, someone who understood the game better than she did.

Someone who could save her from herself.

She stared at Carson Crest, this beautiful predator offering her salvation wrapped in silk and control.

"Where do I sign?"

Carson's smile was triumphant, though something dark glinted in his steel eyes for a moment. He handed her a stylus, his fingers lingering against hers in contact that felt deliberately intimate.

Kinsley signed her name with steady strokes, sealing her fate with digital ink.

"Excellent." Carson tucked the tablet away. "From this moment forward, you belong to me."

The words should have terrified her. Strangely, though, they made her feel safe for the first time in days.

Carson Crest was going to save her life.

She just hoped she'd survive the rescue.

"Come. Let's introduce the world to the new you," he offered his arm to her, and she took it. As Carson guided her back into the ballroom where cameras would capture their first public appearance together, Kinsley realized she didn't care about survival anymore.

She only cared about belonging to the man who promised to make her untouchable.

No matter what that belonging might cost her.

CHAPTER FOUR

CARSON

For years, Carson gathered what he needed to dismantle Kinsley's life, and watching her sign her soul away to him was the most beautiful thing he'd ever seen.

Three days had passed since the gala, and the operation was proceeding flawlessly. His monitors displayed the systematic isolation of Kinsley Ellis in real time. Red pins marked eliminated allies, green pins showed planted assets, yellow dots tracking her movements through the city.

She had no idea she was already his.

But something was wrong with him. Carson should be enjoying this more.

The surveillance feed from her apartment showed Kinsley pacing her living room, phone pressed to her ear as she spoke with her free hand waving around and sloshing wine everywhere. Carson adjusted the audio feed to hear her conversation with her former assistant.

"Kris, please. I just need someone who doesn't think I'm a monster."

Carson pulled up the bot network he'd unleashed on Kristina's social media. Forty-three vicious comments on her latest post, variations of "How could you work for such a fake bitch?" The algorithm pushed the hatred to the top for maximum impact.

"I can't deal with this right now, Kinsley." Kristina's voice carried on speaker phone. "They're targeting me now too. My other clients are asking questions. Some have even backed out. I have to protect my business."

The line went dead. On screen, Kinsley stared at the silent phone, her shoulders shaking as she downed the rest of the wine. If he was keeping track, and he was, that was already half a bottle and it was only one in the afternoon.

Carson waited for the familiar rush of satisfaction. The dark pleasure he'd felt dismantling his other targets. Instead, something twisted uncomfortably in his chest as he watched her break down.

This was what Emma had gone through. The isolation, the betrayal, the slow realization that the world had turned against her. Carson had orchestrated every detail to mirror Emma's final weeks, but watching it unfold made his stomach clench with something that wasn't quite satisfaction.

He opened another file, this one of fabricated screenshots of text conversations between Kinsley and her college roommate, doctored to make it appear Kinsley had been talking behind her back for months. The screenshots had been delivered to Alicia Jones two hours ago, along with an anonymous note: "*Thought you should know what your 'friend' really thinks of you.*"

Alicia's response came quicker than he expected: blocking Kinsley on all platforms and posting a vague but damaging message about "learning people's true colors."

His phone buzzed with updates from the operation. Kinsley's gym membership terminated. Her grocery delivery service flagged her address as problematic. Her other influencer friends had received fabricated photos that made her lawyer recommend cutting contact.

All according to plan. So why couldn't he shake the feeling that he was watching himself destroy something he might want to keep?

A toy he didn't want to break quite yet?

Carson's phone rang. Benedict's name appeared on the screen.

"How's our reputation rehabilitation going with Kinsley Ellis?" Benedict asked, his voice carrying genuine warmth. "I've been monitoring the media coverage. The narrative's shifting in her favor since the gala and the photos that came out about the two of you getting lunch the other day. It's good news on most fronts."

Carson's jaw tightened. Benedict believed they were actually helping Kinsley rebuild her image, not systematically destroying her support system. Carson had fed him and all the others carefully crafted half-truths about "strategic isolation" to eliminate "toxic influences" from her life. Only Tanner had seemed suspicious, but goodness knew he wouldn't say anything. Talking to Tanner Whitney was like talking to a wall with bigger biceps than some tree trunks.

"It seems like our isolation protocol is working," Carson said carefully. "I think it's a good idea to continue removing the people who were exploiting her vulnerability."

"Sure. She certainly seems like a decent person caught in a bad situation. I guess most of our average clients are that way though, and she's friends with Pai, so I shouldn't be surprised. But your sister's really worried about her. She mentioned Kinsley's been withdrawing from everyone lately."

"When did you talk to Paisley?" The line went silent for a second before Benedict answered.

"We crossed paths after the gala the other night. She brought up seeing her. It was a good chat."

"Uh huh." Carson mumbled.

"Anyways, all I'm saying is this is more extreme than normal. Her assistant terminated their professional relationship today. Her college roommate blocked all contact. Her therapist canceled their standing appointments." Benedict paused and sighed. "It just seems like it's more than removing toxic influences.

"What does it seem like, Ben?"

"Creating artificial dependence."

Carson gritted his teeth. "Kinsley needs to understand who she can really trust," Carson replied. "Sometimes that requires removing illusions about people who were never truly loyal."

25

"Carson, what exactly are you doing to her?"

For years, Carson had run Crest Strategies with Benedict before the other three had joined the team. He and Benedict had built their reputation management empire together, and Carson had trusted him with every dark secret of their business.

Except this one.

"I'm helping her rebuild," Carson said. "Sometimes that requires difficult choices about who deserves to be part of her new life."

"She seems... fragile. More dependent than your usual clients. Are you certain she's consenting to this level of life restructuring?"

"She signed the contract."

"Contracts can't consent to psychological manipulation." Benedict's voice hardened. "If you're using Crest Strategies resources for personal vendetta—"

"Careful." Carson's tone dropped to dangerous levels. "You're questioning my judgment."

"I'm questioning your methods. There's a difference between reputation management and systematic isolation."

Carson's grip tightened on the phone. "Rest assured, the isolation on Kinsley is temporary. Once we've cleared out the opportunists, she'll be stronger."

"Fine. I still think this approach is pretty aggressive, but you're the expert on reputation management. Just... make sure we're not isolating her from genuine support, okay? She needs real friends right now."

"Of course." The lie came easily. "I've got work to do. Bye Ben."

Carson ended the call and turned back to the monitors. Kinsley was reading something on her phone now, her face cycling through confusion and hurt. Undoubtedly she was seeing the screenshots he'd leaked this morning—fabricated evidence of her friends taking money to sell stories about her.

She dropped the phone like it had burned her, then curled into a ball on her couch.

Carson's chest tightened, but he pushed the feeling aside. This was justice. He glanced at Emma's photo. His fiancée had suffered the same betrayal, the same isolation. Kinsley deserved to know how it felt.

Even if watching her cry was starting to make him feel sick.

His phone buzzed with a text from Kinsley.

I need you right now. I'm panicking.

Carson stared at the message. Something dark and possessive coiled in his chest, and he didn't understand where it was coming from.

He typed back with one hand, pocketing his keys with the other.

I'll be there soon.

Twenty minutes later, Carson stood outside her apartment building, his hands steadier than they'd been in days. He'd stopped at James's office on the way over and retrieved something that would give Kinsley hope. Real evidence of coordinated attacks, carefully edited to hide his involvement before James even had a chance to look at it.

He knocked on her door. "Kinsley? It's Carson."

The locks turned immediately, and the door opened to reveal Kinsley in an oversized hoodie and booty shorts that barely peeked from under the hem of her sweatshirt. Her eyes were red and swollen from crying. She looked ruffled and flustered. Tired, yes, but ultimately, she looked sexy.

And Carson's body responded immediately.

Blood rushed south as he took in her disheveled appearance, the way the hoodie hung off one shoulder, exposing a stretch of smooth skin. Her vulnerability should have disgusted him, not made him hard. She was the enemy, the woman responsible for Emma's death.

But when she looked at him with desperate relief, Carson wanted to pin her against the wall and claim her mouth until she forgot every cruel word the world had thrown at her.

He hated himself for it.

"Carson." Her voice broke on his name. "Thank god you're here."

She threw her arms around him without thinking, and Carson's body went rigid with shock and arousal. She smelled like cinnamon and wine, warm and soft against his chest. Her breasts pressed against him through the hoodie, and god, she wasn't wearing a bra. Carson had to clench his jaw to keep from groaning.

This was wrong. She was supposed to be his target, not his temptation.

He needed to get fucked soon or his dick would do the thinking for him.

"Hey," he said roughly, his arms coming up to hold her despite every rational thought screaming at him to pull away. "Sorry it took me so long. Traffic was a bitch."

Kinsley pulled back, wiping her eyes, apparently oblivious to the effect she was having on him. "I'm sorry to call you over so unexpectedly. I just... everything's falling apart. Everyone's abandoning me, and I don't understand why. I thought things were getting better."

Carson forced a concern look, or at least, what he hoped was a concerned look. It could've, by all rights, made him look constipated. He took the gamble anyways. "Tell me what's happening."

She led him to her living room, and Carson couldn't help but notice the way her hips swayed beneath the loose fabric. When she gestured at her phone on the coffee table, her hoodie rode up slightly, exposing a strip of toned stomach that made his mouth go dry.

Fuck. He wanted to bend her over the back of that couch and pound into her until she was screaming his name as she came on his cock.

What the hell?

Focus. She killed Emma. She deserved everything that was happening to her.

"Look at this. Alicia, my old roommate, even my trainer. They're all taking money to sell stories about me. Stories about how awful I am."

Carson picked up her phone and scrolled through the screenshots, his expression carefully neutral. The fabricated evidence looked convincing even to him. "This definitely seems systematic."

"That's what I thought. Someone's orchestrating this, right? But I can't figure out who or why. I just...I feel so alone."

Carson set the phone down and pulled an envelope from his jacket. "Actually, I might have some answers for you."

Kinsley's eyes widened. "What's that?"

"I had my team do some digging after we signed our contract. Call it due diligence." Carson handed her the envelope, watching her face carefully. "We found evidence of a coordinated attack on your reputation. As we suspected, someone's been planning this for a long time."

It was true, technically. Just not the someone she thought.

Kinsley opened the envelope with shaking hands and pulled out a series of documents; real evidence of bot networks and paid trolls, carefully edited to remove any connection to Carson's operation.

"Oh my god." Her voice was barely a whisper. "This is... this is insane. Who would do this to me? Why? What did I do to deserve this kind of...this kind of..."

"Hate?"

"Oh god." Kinsley's face crumpled.

Carson moved closer, close enough to catch her scent again, close enough to feel the heat radiating from her body. His proximity was meant to be protective and reassuring, but all it did was make him want to back her against the wall and show her exactly how much power he had over her.

"Someone with resources and a personal vendetta is doing this. We're still investigating, but I wanted you to know you're not paranoid. This is real."

Kinsley looked up at him with such hurt and confused gratitude that something twisted in Carson's chest. "Thank you"

"Don't thank me yet. Remember, I'm going to help you fight back."

Kinsley's smile was small, but seemed real.

Carson smiled back, even as a twinge of self-loathing crawled up his spine. He was supposed to be destroying her, not wanting to protect her. Supposed to be avenging Emma, not getting hard from holding his enemy while she cried.

But as he watched light return to her dull eyes, Carson realized he was in deeper trouble than he'd ever imagined.

He still wanted to destroy Kinsley Ellis.

He just wasn't sure anymore if it was for Emma's sake or because he was starting to want her in ways that had nothing to do with revenge.

And that terrified him.

CHAPTER FIVE

KINSLEY

THE FAKE DATING CAMPAIGN WAS WORKING BETTER THAN Kinsley could've ever had hoped. It'd been three weeks since Carson had come over and shown her the proof that someone was trying to ruin her. Three weeks of carefully orchestrated public appearances. Dinners at exclusive restaurants where paparazzi happened to be waiting. Gallery openings where they were photographed gazing into each other's eyes. A carefully leaked story about Carson "helping Kinsley heal from the trauma of systematic cyberbullying."

The media had eaten it up. *"Billionaire's Faith Saves Fallen Influencer."* *"Second Chance Romance: How Carson Crest Saw the Real Kinsley Ellis."* *"Love Conquers Cancel Culture."* For the first time, it didn't feel like there was gigantic weight resting on her chest.

Actually, there wasn't much of anything on her chest at the moment. Or her body. In fact, she felt almost naked.

That part she wasn't so keen on.

Kinsley had never needed anyone's approval more than she needed Carson's, which should have terrified her.

She stared at her reflection in the makeup trailer at the Tribeca Photography studio mirror, trying to steady her breathing. Three weeks of Carson orchestrating her every move, managing her social media, controlling every aspect of her carefully crafted comeback. He'd moved fast—canceling her remaining obligations, rescheduling everything, building a fortress of protection around her shattered reputation.

And somewhere in that time, she'd started living for Carson's quiet nods of satisfaction.

Apparently, a luxury jewelry brand had specifically requested her for their new campaign. It seemed like a good testament to how successfully Crest Strategies had rehabilitated her image already.

"Five minutes, Ms. Ellis," the photographer's assistant called through the trailer door.

Kinsley smoothed her hands over the silk slip dress that barely qualified as clothing. The brand had specifically requested something "intimate but elegant" for their new campaign, and Carson had insisted she take the job.

The makeup artist applied one final coat of gloss to her lips, the nude pink shade chosen personally by Carson. He'd been making all her aesthetic decisions lately; what she wore, how she styled her hair, even the angle of her photos. It wasn't as suffocating as she would've thought. It felt more like letting go and giving the decisions to someone who had the energy to make them.

It was nice.

Kinsley stepped out of the trailer into the converted warehouse studio, immediately scanning for Carson's familiar silhouette. She found him standing with the photographer near an elaborate bed setup, his charcoal suit immaculate as always.

Their eyes met across the room, and something warm unfurled in her chest. Carson's gaze traveled from her face down to her bare legs, lingering where silk clung to her curves. When his eyes returned to hers, a flicker of something darker flashed before his professional mask slipped back into place.

Carson sauntered over while the photographer continued speaking to an assistant in French.

"Nervous?" Carson asked.

"Excited." Kinsley beamed at him despite the insecurity trickling through her. She wasn't the smallest woman, and she started second guessing whether the dress—if she could even call it a dress—covered enough skin. But she hid the concern behind her smile. "Three weeks ago, I couldn't get a brand to return my calls. Now I'm the face of a beautiful new collection."

"Good. The photographer is Gabriel Dubois," Carson said, giving her another satisfied once over. "He's worked with every major fashion house. This campaign will cement your comeback."

"Thank you," Kinsley said, her hand settling on his arm. "None of this would have happened without you."

Heat traveled through the palm of her hand, and she cleared her throat, pulling back. Three weeks of playing the devoted girlfriend, and her body had started believing the performance. When he smiled at her like he was her knight in shining armor, when he pressed close to her for photographs and tucked strands of hair behind her ear, when he looked at her with dark lust in his eyes, she struggled to remember that it was all for show. It was fake.

Carson Crest wasn't really hers.

"Kinsley, darling!" The photographer, Gabriel, waving his very expensive looking camera around as he gestured. "You look absolutely divine. Carson's vision for this campaign is pure genius." He moved quickly towards Kinsley, kissing her on both cheeks. She stilled, glancing to Carson, whose demeanor had darkened.

"It's nice to meet you, Mr. DuBois."

Gabriel clapped his hands together. "Wonderful! Let's begin with some solo shots on the bed, then we'll bring in the male model for the couple's portion."

Kinsley's stomach dropped. "Male model?"

Carson's expression didn't change, but she caught the way his jaw tightened almost imperceptibly. "Gabriel, that won't be necessary. I'll work with Kinsley for the couple shots myself."

"Oh?" Gabriel's eyebrows rose with interest.

"It will feel more authentic that way," Carson continued smoothly, wrapping an arm around Kinsley's waist and pulling her close. Her heart flipped. "More natural chemistry."

The way he'd inserted himself into her shoot should have surprised her. Instead, relief flooded her system. The thought of a stranger's hands on her while Carson watched had made her uncomfortable in ways she couldn't name.

"Brilliant!" Gabriel practically bounced with excitement. "You two do have incredible energy together. This will be much better."

Kinsley's cheeks warmed as Gabriel and his assistants began arranging lights around the bed. She wasn't a professional model. This was her first high-fashion shoot in several years, and her first on a bed. The idea of being photographed in lingerie was nerve-wracking enough without adding Carson to the equation.

"Still excited?" Carson appeared beside her, close enough that she could smell his cologne.

"Yes, though..." she paused, biting her lip. "I've never done anything this... intimate."

"Don't worry, sweetheart. I'll talk you through it." His steady warm hand settled on the small of her back. "Keep your eyes on me when you get nervous."

The simple contact sent comfort cascading through her chest. Carson had become her anchor in a world that still felt hostile. He shielded her from cruel comments and made her feel valuable again when everything else felt broken.

"Alright, let's start simple," Gabriel called out. "Kinsley, if you could lie on the bed. Think sultry but innocent. Carson, you'll join her in a moment."

Kinsley climbed onto the massive four-poster bed, hyperaware of how the silk dress rode up her thighs. The sheets were cool against her skin and she shivered. Gabriel snapped at least four hundred photos, giving helpful instruction along the way.

"Beautiful, darling! Now arch your back slightly—perfect. Carson, come stand at the foot of the bed."

Carson removed his suit jacket and rolled up his sleeves, revealing strong forearms. When he positioned himself where Gabriel directed, his eyes never left hers, steady and reassuring.

"Excellent. Beautiful," Gabriel murmured, camera clicking rapidly. "Carson, move closer. Rest one knee on the bed."

The mattress dipped under Carson's weight as he leaned over her. This close and with the harsh lighting, silver flecks sparkled in his steel-gray eyes. Warmth radiated from his body.

"Look at him like you trust him completely," Gabriel instructed. "Like he's your safe harbor."

That was easy. Carson had become exactly that.

"Perfect," Gabriel breathed. "Now Carson, touch her face. Gentle, like she's precious."

Carson's hand cupped her cheek, his thumb tracing along her jawline. The touch was soft, careful, but something in his eyes made her pulse quicken.

"Just breathe," he murmured, so quietly only she could hear. "You're doing so well."

God, did she have a praise kink?

She had to, because her stomach heated into something molten and she had to clench her thighs for a moment.

The camera clicked frantically as Gabriel captured the moment, but Kinsley barely noticed. All her attention focused on Carson's hand against her skin, the way his gaze never wavered from hers.

"Now lean down, Carson. Almost kissing but not quite. Create tension."

Carson braced himself above Kinsley, his face inches from hers. His scent surrounded her, an expensive cologne mixed with something uniquely him that made her want to breathe deeper.

"Eyes on me," he said softly, his voice rougher than usual.

This close, she could see every detail of his face. The sharp line of his jaw, the way his dark hair fell across his forehead, the steady pulse at his throat. Something about his proximity made her feel both protected and exposed.

"Beautiful!" Gabriel called out. "Now Carson, put your hand on her throat. Gentle."

Oh. Oh god.

The heat tripled in her stomach and she could feel her face flushing.

Carson's hand moved to her neck, fingers spanning her throat. He grinned down at her. The touch of his hand on her made her feel claimed in a way that sent a tremor through her entire body.

"I can feel your pulse," Carson observed, his voice dropping lower. "Racing."

The way he said it made her breathing shallow. "I know."

"You like this, don't you, Kinsley?" His thumb stroked over her pulse point.

"Yes," she whispered.

"Magnificent!" Gabriel's voice seemed to come from very far away. "The intensity is incredible. Let's try something more intimate."

The next twenty minutes passed in a careful dance of increasingly close poses. Carson's hands guided her body with growing confidence, his touch becoming more deliberate. And his voice—god, his voice kept dropping into that rough register that made her want to lean into him. Press back into him. Sink onto him.

"Turn just like that. Perfect."

"Look at me. Just me."

"Fuck, you're gorgeous."

"Bend over more. Let me see those perfect tits."

Each instruction sent need spiraling through her, and she responded to him in ways that had nothing to do with the camera.

"Excellent work, both of you," Gabriel said, reviewing images on a screen off to the side. "The chemistry is electric. Take fifteen minutes, then we'll finish with some outdoor shots."

Carson helped Kinsley off the bed, his hand lingering at her waist. The moment they were away from the cameras, he stepped closer, close enough that she had to tilt her head back to look at him.

"How are you feeling?" he asked, his voice still carrying that low, intimate tone.

"Like I need water," she admitted. "And like...like you see more of me than anyone else ever has."

Carson's eyes darkened. "I am. I do. And I like what I'm seeing."

His hand trailed up her arm slowly. "You're more responsive than I expected."

The word choice made her core clench. This was supposed to be fake dating. Strategic positioning. But Carson was looking at her like he wanted to devour her, and she was responding like she wanted to let him.

Maybe she deserved a little fun. Paisley had suggested it at the gala, right? Maybe after everything she'd been through, she was allowed to want something easy and hot. Even if it was complicated.

"Carson..." she started, then deliberately stepped closer, watching his pupils dilate. "What if I told you I was thinking about your hands? About how they feel on my skin?"

Carson's grip on her arm tightened, his breathing shifting. "I'd say that's dangerous territory."

"Is it? Are you dangerous?" She moved another inch closer, enough to see the exact moment his control started to fray.

"Don't ask stupid questions."

"Are you?"

"Yes."

"What if I told you I want you to keep touching me? Even after the cameras stop?"

Carson's jaw clenched, his eyes blazing with something that made her want to drop to her knees for him there. "Then I'd say you're playing with fire."

"Maybe I want to get burned." The boldness of her own words surprised her, but she was tired of being careful. Tired of being the victim. If Carson wanted to play games during the photoshoot, she could play too.

For a moment, something predatory flashed across his features—something that reminded her this man was dangerous in ways that had nothing to do with her reputation.

"Careful," he murmured, his voice dropping to a register that made her thighs clench. "You have no idea what you're asking for."

Before she could respond, Gabriel called them back to work.

The outdoor portion of the shoot took place on the building's rooftop, and everything changed the moment Carson positioned himself behind her.

"Think about what you just told me," he murmured against her ear as Gabriel adjusted lighting again, Carson's chest pressed against her back.

Kinsley leaned into him deliberately and froze when she felt something hard and unmistakable pressing against her lower back. Carson was aroused. Very aroused.

The realization sent electricity through her entire body and she pressed into his erection, but before she could process it fully, Carson's hands tightened on her waist in warning.

"Don't move like that unless you're prepared for the consequences," he breathed, his voice strained.

She turned her head slightly, just enough to catch his eye. "What if I am?"

Kinsley circled her hips once.

Carson's grip tightened. "Then you're about to find out how much trouble you're in."

"Excellent positioning, you two!" Gabriel called out, completely oblivious to the tension crackling between them. "Carson, can you lean down and whisper something in her ear? Like you're telling her a secret?"

Carson's lips brushed her ear as he spoke, his voice so low only she could hear. "You think you're in control right now. But I can feel how you're trembling. I can hear how your breathing changed when you pressed against me. You'd beg for me, and we both know it."

Kinsley's pulse hammered, but she lifted her chin. "I can feel how hard you are. So who's really in control?"

Carson's laugh was dark and dangerous. "Oh, sweetheart. You have no idea what you've just started."

His hand moved to her throat again, fingers spanning her neck. To Gabriel and the crew, it looked like he was performing for the camera, highlighting the necklace they'd put her in. But Carson's thumb traced patterns against her pulse that made her knees weak.

"Feel that?" he murmured, his lips still at her ear. "How fast your heart is beating? Your body knows exactly who's in charge here. I bet if I stuck my hands between your legs, I'd get soaked."

He wasn't wrong.

Kinsley tried to maintain her composure, but when Carson's other hand settled low on her hip, his fingers brushing the edge of her silk dress, her breathing stuttered.

"Beautiful!" Gabriel called out. "The intimacy is perfect. Can you look back at him, Kinsley? Like he just told you something that made you want him?"

She turned in Carson's arms, and the heat in his eyes nearly undid her. This close, she could see the careful control he was exercising, the way his jaw was clenched with the effort of maintaining professional boundaries while his body betrayed exactly what he wanted to do to her.

"You're beautiful when you're worked up," he said quietly, his thumb stroking along her jawline. "But I bet you're even more beautiful when your boneless and satisfied from a good fuck."

"Why don't you find out."

Carson's smile was pure predator. "I intend to."

For the next series of shots, Carson systematically destroyed her composure with touches that looked innocent to the camera. His fingers traced along her spine, making her arch into him, his large erection covered by her ass. His hand cupped her face while his thumb brushed dangerously close to her lips. God, what would it be like to suck his fingers while he made her climax?

When Gabriel directed them to lie on a blanket together, Carson positioned himself above her, his body caging her in while he whispered instructions that had nothing to do with photography.

"This is the best view of you. Beneath me, half naked. Spread your fingers on my chest. That's it. Now imagine what it would feel like if my hand was between your legs."

"Bite your lip for me. Just like that. Fuck that mouth is perfect."

"Arch your back. Show me how beautiful you look when you want something."

Each command sent her spiraling higher and higher, and Kinsley obeyed, her earlier boldness dissolving under the weight of his focused attention. He was in control, and by the smirk on his lips and the lust in his eyes, he knew it.

By the time Gabriel called the final shot, Kinsley was breathing hard and completely undone. Carson had turned the tables on her so smoothly she hadn't even realized she was losing until it was too late.

"Magnificent work, both of you," Gabriel said, beaming as he reviewed the final images. "The chemistry is absolutely electric. These are going to be stunning."

Carson helped Kinsley to her feet, his hand hot on her waist.

"Thank you, Gabriel. I think we got exactly what we needed," he said. As the crew began breaking down equipment, Carson leaned close to her ear. "You started something up here, sweetheart. Are you ready to finish it?"

Kinsley's response caught in her throat. She'd thought she could play his game, but Carson had just shown her exactly how outmatched she was. And the most terrifying part was how much she wanted to let him win.

She wanted him in control.

Craved it.

"We should celebrate this shoot," Carson said as they walked toward his car, his voice carrying that commanding undertone that made her pulse race. "Somewhere private."

Kinsley's pulse was still erratic as they walked out to Carson's Corvette. The way Carson had touched her, spoken to her, during the photoshoot had shaken her. She slid into the passenger seat when he opened the door for her, already missing the weight of his body against hers, the promise in his touch.

Carson sat in the drivers seat and buckled his seatbelt. "All that touching got you worked up, didn't it?"

Heat flooded her cheeks. "Maybe."

"No maybes. It's a yes or a no. Are you wet for me right now?"

"I—yes."

Admitting it out loud seemed to confirm something for him and a smirk played at the corners of his mouth.

Carson reached over to tuck a stray curl behind her ear. "You're beautiful when you blush." His thumb brushed her cheek, sending a shiver down her spine. "I bet your even more beautiful with mascara running down your cheeks and my dick in your mouth."

"I—" She had no doubt she'd choke if the hardness she'd felt pressed against her during the photoshoot was any indication of his size. "Um." She cleared her throat, trying to regain her composure. "So, dinner?"

A playful glint shone in his eyes. "First, I believe you owe me an apology."

She blinked. "An apology?"

His fingers trailed down her neck, over her collarbone, and lower, until her breath caught in her throat. "You challenged me back there. Suggested you wanted to take control. That's dangerous territory."

She swallowed hard as his hand paused just above her breast, his finger tracing lazy patterns through the air above her silk dress. "I... guess I wasn't expecting you to handle it so well."

His finger finally made contact, circling her nipple through the delicate fabric. He leaned in close, his lips brushing her earlobe as he whispered, "I plan to handle you *very* well, Kinsley Ellis."

Her breath hitched, and a wave of dampness pooled between her legs. No doubt in her mind; this man would make her beg without even trying.

Carson pulled back, straightening in his seat as he put the car in drive. "Now, I think we need to establish some rules."

Kinsley's heart began to pound again. "Rules?"

His eyes remained on the road as he asked casually, "One rule, actually. Have you ever played this game before, sweetheart? Submission and control?"

She shook her head, unable to form words as he smoothed his hand up her thigh. "No."

A low hum rumbled in his chest. "Good. That means I get to teach you exactly how I like to play."

His hand continued its slow path up her leg, her skirt inching higher and higher. "My rule: Nothing happens unless you ask for it. Explicitly."

Kinsley's chest tightened as his fingers edged closer, teasing the sensitive skin on the inside of her thigh. "Ask for what?" she managed to breathe.

"Anything and everything." He pulled his hand away, leaving her wanting. "Be specific. Tell me where and how you want to be touched. And if you're very good, I might just give it to you."

She bit her lip. "And if I don't ask?"

His eyes flicked to hers for less than a second, but it was long enough to see how sharp they were. "Then you don't get a damn thing." He caught her staring in the review mirror. "Do we continue? Do you agree?"

"Yes." The word came quickly, and she blushed again. She knew she should've been embarrassed for how fast the response had left her lips, but it'd been so long since another man had touched her like this. Too long.

Carson's hand returned, his long fingers smoothing over her thigh. "I bet you're already dripping for me. Tell me, was it because of the photoshoot? Because I got you so worked up you can't stand it?"

She couldn't form a coherent sentence, could only nod.

"Tell me, Kinsley." His finger traced patterns on her inner thigh, dangerously close to the center of her desire. "Say the words."

"I... it's because of you."

"That's my girl." His hand finally continued its path towards where she wanted him most. Just a bit more, and... he stopped. She tried to adjust so it would be closer, but he pulled away.

"I told you the main rule, and now I want you to repeat it back to me."

"What?"

"What's the rule, Kinsley?"

She frowned, distracted by the absence of his hand.

"Kinsley." He squeezed her thigh.

"I have to ask explicitly."

"Good girl, now ask." Carson's fingers moved back and hovered just above her core through the silk.

She swallowed, the request sticking in her throat.

He smiled, but his eyes, which were focused on the road, were dark. "You want this, don't you?"

She nodded, breathless.

His finger circled lightly just above her clit through the silk, making her back arch in response. "Use your words, Kinsley."

"Please... touch me." Her voice was little more than a whisper.

"Where?" He raised an eyebrow. "Explicitly, sweetheart. That's the rule."

"My clit."

Carson hummed his approval, his finger now pressing directly onto the most sensitive part. "Good girl."

His thumb joined, his fingers worked her into a frenzy. She bit her lip to stifle her moans, but Carson seemed to read her body like an open book, using pressure and motion to bring her to the very edge. All the while, his other hand never left the steering wheel.

Kinsley's head fell back against the seat, her breathing turning shallow as Carson's fingers found exactly the right pressure, the right rhythm. The fabric between them was torture and salvation at once.

"Look at you," he murmured, keeping his eyes on the road while his fingers worked her. "So responsive for me. So good."

The combination of his touch and his voice overwhelmed her completely. Kinsley pressed closer to his hand, desperate for more contact, more pressure, more of whatever he was willing to give her.

"Please," she whispered without meaning to.

Carson's chuckle was pure predator. "Please what? Tell me what you want."

"I want—" The words evaporated as he pressed more firmly against her, making coherent thought impossible.

He didn't relent. "Why should I give you what you want, Kinsley? What have you done to earn it?"

Earn it? Her mind raced as her body begged for more. "I—I'll do anything."

"Anything?" His voice was velvet roughness. "Then prove it." His thumb circled her clit once, twice, then paused. "Look at me and say my name. Tell me I own you."

Her pulse hammered at the erotic demand, but his fingers stilled, waiting.

She swallowed. "Carson. Please, Carson."

He rewarded her with a slow stroke, sending lightning through her core. "Say it, Kinsley. Tell me I own you."

The confession ripped from her. "You own me. Please, just—oh god."

She squirmed under his touch, his fingers seeming to know exactly where to apply pressure, exactly how to push her closer to the edge. "Carson, fuck..."

"I could make you come right here in my car," he said conversationally, as if discussing the weather instead of driving her out of her mind. "And you'd let me, wouldn't you?"

Kinsley could only whimper in response, her body betraying exactly how close she was to falling apart under his touch. Every muscle was beginning to coil tight as he drove her higher and higher.

"Answer me," Carson commanded softly. "Would you let me make you come in my car?"

"Yes," she gasped, beyond caring how desperate she sounded.

"Good girl." The praise sent electricity straight through her core. "But not yet," he instructed, his voice commanding. "Not until I say so."

She was completely at his mercy, but instead of scaring her, it sent her higher.

He spoke in a low voice, words that made her ache. "Don't you dare finish."

"Carson, fuck, I'm so close, please—"

He chuckled, his fingers relentless. "Not yet."

She squirmed, desperation building. Just a bit more pressure and she knew she'd see the stars she so desperately craved. "Please, I need to—"

He suddenly withdrew, leaving her aching and empty. "You don't get to come until I say so. Remember?"

She whimpered, frantically searching for his hand. This man had just brought her to the brink, and now he left her hanging, needy, and completely under his control. She lowered her hand to finish the job, but he grabbed her wrist in a firm grasp and yanked it towards him.

"No," he growled. "You're mine, remember? Mine to rile. Mine to finish. You don't get to play with yourself anymore. Is that clear? Mine. Say it."

Kinsley wanted to complain. To moan. To beg him to finish her then. But instead, she nodded her head. "Yours."

Carson removed his hand from her wrist just as they pulled into the restaurant's valet area, leaving her aching and desperate and completely undone.

"We're here," he said, straightening his tie as if he hadn't just driven her to the edge of madness with nothing but his fingers and his voice.

Kinsley stared at him, breathless and flushed and throbbing with need, realizing that Carson Crest had just claimed ownership of her body without her even noticing.

And they hadn't even made it to dinner yet.

CHAPTER SIX

CARSON

CARSON WATCHED KINSLEY STRUGGLE TO COMPOSE herself as the valet opened her door, her legs unsteady as she stood. He grinned. He'd done that. She'd let him. No, she'd *begged* him, and her moans and cries had gone entirely to his head. Both of them. His erection throbbed, but he was going to let her finish until he was ready to take her like he wanted. Like she deserved. Rough and without an ounce of mercy.

For now, though, they'd both have to wait.

The flush still stained Kinsley's cheeks. Her breathing hadn't quite returned to normal, and she pressed her thighs together, seeking relief he'd deliberately denied her.

Perfect. She was exactly as desperate, dependent, and needy as he had wanted her to be.

Carson handed his keys to the valet and placed his hand on the small of Kinsley's back, guiding her toward the restaurant entrance. The simple touch made her shiver, and his cock responded in turn. Fuck, he wanted her. Four and a half years of watching her, and he was getting hard from her reactions instead of her destruction.

Maybe something was wrong. Maybe this had turned into something more than revenge.

He shoved the annoying thought out of his head. He was just horny and she had been breathing hard for him all day. Carson forced his focus onto her.

"You okay?" he murmured against her ear as they approached the hostess stand.

Kinsley's breath caught. "I'm fine."

"Liar." His fingers pressed into her spine. "You're still wet, aren't you? Dripping."

The way she bit her lip confirmed everything he suspected. Good. Let her be distracted. Let her crave him so completely that she'd forget to question his motives.

"Mr. Crest," the hostess greeted them. "Your table is ready."

Carson had specifically requested a corner booth. It gave them the intimate privacy he needed to continue to drive the woman beside him wild. As they were seated, he deliberately chose the spot beside Kinsley instead of across from her, his thigh pressing against hers under the table.

"The wine list, sir?" their server asked.

"We'll have the 2015 Barolo," Carson said without consulting Kinsley. "And we'll need a few minutes with the menu."

Carson's phone buzzed with a text from Benedict.

> Something's happening, C. What were you doing with the Ashford case?

Benedict could wait. The way Kinsley's eyes darkened when he slid his hand under the table to rest on her knee was far more interesting than whatever crisis his business partner was handling.

"So," he said, voice dropping to that register he knew made her pulse quicken. "Tell me about your childhood. What was little Kinsley Ellis like before she became social media's darling?"

Kinsley laughed, the sound genuine enough to catch him off guard. "Loud. Opinionated. My parents were constantly telling me to be quieter and more polite." She took a sip of water. "I had this phase where I'd correct adults when they were wrong about something. My mother was mortified."

Carson's phone buzzed again. He silenced it without looking.

"You? Confrontational? I can't imagine." He squeezed her knee, watching goosebumps rise on her arms. "What happened to that girl?"

Something vulnerable flickered across her face. "She posted her first video at fourteen. The comments section happened."

His phone vibrated three times in rapid succession. Irritation prickled under his skin.

"Excuse me," he muttered, finally glancing down.

Benedict's second text left his stomach uneasy.

> Emergency. Ashford situation escalated.

Fuck. He'd thought he'd dealt with Ashford. Before Kinsley's fall from grace, that had been his focus; keeping the ghosts of his business in the past where they belonged. Now the Ashford mess was resurfacing. Fucking perfect. When they'd taken Ashford down three years ago, Carson had handled that situation personally and dismantled Richard Ashford's empire piece by piece after discovering the man's corruption. The rat deserved it, selling US secrets to enemies outside the States.

The suicide afterward had been... unfortunate, but not Carson's problem.

Tanner's message followed.

> Crest, someone is making statements about us. You need to come in.

No. What he needed to do was get Kinsley on her hands and knees and get her back to begging.

That's what he needed.

Carson kept his expression neutral as he set his phone face-down. "Sorry about that. Work never stops."

"Everything okay?" Kinsley asked, her head tilting as her gaze traveled over his face. He held his mask in place, even offering her an apologetic smile.

48

"Nothing I can't handle." He flagged down their server. "Another glass of wine?"

"Of course." Kinsley nodded, but she studied him with more perception than he'd given her credit for. "You just look tense all of the sudden."

"I'm just thinking of spreading you out on this table and taking you in front of everyone."

Kinsley's breathing quickened, and her nipples tightened beneath the silk of her dress.

"Carson..." she whispered.

"I'm going to use my tongue first," he continued, his voice so low only she could hear. "Lick you until you're begging me to stop, then keep going until you scream. Think they'll appreciate that?"

Her hand trembled against his leg, and Carson smiled with dark satisfaction. This was power, reducing her to desperate need with nothing but words.

His phone vibrated again, this time skittering slightly across the table's surface. It was Benedict.

> I'm doing damage control, but we have clients that are furious about what's being said, Cars. Please answer!

Carson ignored it, focusing instead on the curve of Kinsley's neck, the way her collarbone peeked from beneath her blouse. He'd spent four and a half years watching her, imagining her broken and begging. Now that she was here, dependent on him, he wasn't going to throw it away on a work problem his other four highly capable business partners should know how to handle.

"Tell me more about your parents," he said, deliberately steering away from work. Compared to the declaration that he wanted to eat her out in front of the restaurant, the change in topics seemed a bit like whiplash. "Are you close?"

Kinsley's expression clouded. "We were. Until the scandal. My mother thinks I've embarrassed the family name. I guess I have."

The wine tasted bitter when a second ago it had been fine. Carson frowned. "You lost relationship with your family because of this." It was information he knew. Information he'd orchestrated through the fake bots and internet trolls. Yet, seeing the hurt on her face didn't resonate the same as it used to.

Though he wasn't as close to his parents as he'd once been, he knew they still loved him and were proud of him. And his relationship with his sister was one of the most important in his life, even if she was busy with her philanthropy work most weeks.

For the first time since he'd sent the message to Kinsley as she fell apart on her bathroom floor, ready to end things like the woman he'd loved, Carson felt a sliver of regret.

The server thankfully arrived a second later to save him from the new uncomfortable feeling spreading through his chest. She offered them fresh wine and took their dinner orders. Carson ordered for them both, but noticed with satisfaction that Kinsley seemed impressed with his ability to know what she wanted without asking.

"Lobster risotto, light on the garlic, extra parmesan," he finished, watching Kinsley's large eyes widen.

"How did you know that's exactly what I wanted?"

His phone buzzed again.

Penn this time.

> You need to see this, Carson.

"I pay attention," Carson replied, ignoring the device. "I see you, Kinsley. Remember?"

Something about her answering smile made his chest tighten. It was too genuine, too appreciative. This wasn't how it was supposed to go. She was supposed to be a target, not a person with dimples that appeared when she smiled at him like that.

"Thank you. For believing in me when no one else does."

I'm the one destroying you, he thought. *I'm the monster you should be running from.*

Instead, he lifted her hand to his lips and pressed a kiss to her knuckles. "You're stronger than they know."

His phone lit up with another message as James joined the conversation.

> I'm handling the legal side, but we need to get in front of this.

Carson took a long swallow of wine. The Ashford situation wasn't the first secret destruction case that had tried to come back to slaughter them, but all the others had been eliminated quickly and quietly. And that's what Carson had been doing.

Before her.

"You're distracted," Kinsley observed, her voice softer than he expected. "Is work really that bad right now?" She ran a hand along his thigh as he had done to her earlier, and he covered her small hand with his large one, moving it higher until she was near enough to stroke his hardening cock through his pants. God, she felt amazing even through the fabric. His mind flashed an image of what she'd look like with his cock gripped in her smaller hands. He let out a low grunt.

Carson met her eyes, surprised by the genuine concern he found there. "Nothing I can't fix," he said.

"Or, maybe I could fix it." The lustful look she gave him nearly undid him.

Carson's breath hitched as Kinsley slipped her hand from his, her fingers tracing the length of him through his pants. His cock throbbed under her touch, and he clenched his jaw to keep from groaning out loud. This woman was going to be the death of him.

"Maybe you can," he murmured, leaning in so his lips brushed her ear. "Take out my dick, Kinsley."

Her cheeks flushed, but she didn't back down. Instead, she unzipped his pants, her hand slipping inside to wrap around his cock. He was rock hard, pulsing in her grip, and it took every ounce of his self-control not to thrust into her hand right there.

"Fuck," he growled, his voice barely above a whisper.

She leaned in, her breath hot on his ear. "Tell me what you want."

He chuckled at her repeating his rule back to her. "Take your hand

and stroke me until I'm coming all over the underside of this table. And so help me, if you play with me, you will regret it."

She stroked him once, then stopped with a dark glint in her eyes. "Are you saying you'll punish me?"

Carson reached down and gripped her wrist, moving her hand along his erection. "Yes. Good girls get to finish."

Apparently that was the motivation she needed.

Her hand began to move, stroking him slowly, torturously. It was dry though, but before he could give her a command, Kinsley glanced around to check if anyone was watching before bending over to spit on the head of his dick.

Fuck. He wanted to grip her by the back of the head and force her to take the length of him, but that would likely draw more attention.

Heat began to build, the tension coiling at the base of his spine. Carson leaned into her, his lips brushing her neck as he whispered filth into her ear.

"You feel that? That's what you do to me. You make me so fucking hard, Kinsley. I want to bend you over this table and fuck you right here, right now. I want to hear you scream my name while everyone watches."

She let out a soft moan, her hand moving faster. Wetness leaked at his tip. She used her thumb to spread the pre-cum around, slipping faster. Gripping harder. Fuck. He was close, so close.

When she leaned over, her tongue darting out to lick the head of his cock, he nearly lost it.

"Fuck, Kinsley," he hissed, his hand gripping her hair. "You're going to make me come right here."

She looked up at him, her eyes dark with desire. "Isn't that the point?"

He chuckled, a low, husky sound. "Do it."

Kinsley twisted her hand as she stroked him and fuck if it didn't make him thrust upwards.

His phone buzzed again. He ignored it, his focus solely on the woman in front of him, on the hand wrapped around his cock, on the sparks building in his gut. But the phone buzzed again, and again, and finally, with a growl of frustration, he pulled it out of his pocket.

Benedict's name flashed on the screen, and Carson's stomach dropped. It was bad.

"Fuck," he muttered, grabbing Kinsley's wrist to make her stop. He wanted to punch the wall. Instead, he released Kinsley, grabbed the cloth napkin and began cleaning her hand off.

Kinsley looked at him, concern etched on her face. "What's wrong? Did I—"

"You didn't do anything wrong. Benedict says there's a crisis going on at work. It..." He glanced down at his already softening erection. "It interrupted at the wrong time."

He finished with her hand and then cleaned himself off, zipping up his pants as discreetly as possible.

"Are you sure it wasn't me?"

Carson caught the worried look in her eyes, and took a deep breath, drawing the hand that had nearly just made him lose his mind in the restaurant up to his lips, where he brushed a soft kiss across her knuckles.

"Trust me, sweetheart. This doesn't end here."

Their food arrived then, the waiter oblivious to what had just happened. Or if she did know, she was exceptional at discretion and certainly deserved a large tip. Carson glanced sidelong at Kinsley, her cheeks still flushed, her breath still coming in quick gasps. He wanted to drag her into the bathroom, to fuck her on the sink, to finish what they'd started. But the moment had passed.

And then the phone buzzed. Again.

It was from Benedict.

Carson, answer your DAMN PHONE!

His screen lit up with a notification that couldn't be ignored: a news alert from The Wall Street Journal mentioning Crest Strategies.

"Shit," he muttered, finally picking up the device.

"What is it?" Kinsley asked, her fork paused midway to her mouth.

"It really is a work emergency." He scrolled quickly through the messages, his jaw tightening. Someone was making very public, very specific allegations about Crest Strategies' methods. About the Ashford case specifically. "Damn it. I'm sorry, but I need to handle this."

Kinsley set down her fork, concern evident in her expression. "Of course. Do you need to go?"

The understanding in her voice made him pause. She should be angry, frustrated by the interruption. Instead, she looked worried for him. It was disarming in a way he hadn't prepared for.

"I do," he admitted, signaling the server. "Can we get these boxed to go, please? And the check."

"Is there anything I can do?" Kinsley asked as they waited.

Carson shook his head, uncomfortable with her kindness. "No, this is... complicated. Business matters that need immediate attention."

The server returned with their packaged meals and the bill, which Carson paid without looking at the amount. He tipped the waitress well, apologizing for dining and dashing. As they left the restaurant, he returned his hand to the small of Kinsley's back. It felt right there. Like she was his. His to guide and protect.

No. That wasn't right. She wasn't someone to protect. She was a target. The enemy. The woman who'd stood by while Emma spiraled.

Wasn't she?

In the car, Kinsley sat quietly beside him, her presence somehow both calming and unsettling. His phone continued to buzz with messages from his partners.

"I'll drop you at my place," he said as they pulled away from the restaurant. "I need to go to the office, but I shouldn't be too long."

"Your place?" she asked, surprise evident in her voice.

"It's closer to my office, and I'm not finished with you yet."

"Good."

Carson's grip tightened on the steering wheel. It was certainly reassuring that she was just as eager as him. It'd been a long time since he'd had a partner as willing to submit as Kinsley.

Still though, frustration crawled up his spine and wrapped itself tightly around his shoulders. This wasn't going according to plan. Not the plan to ruin her. Not the plan to seduce her. Not even the damn plan to keep Ashford buried where he belonged.

Even dinner had been ruined, and he fucking loved steak.

Carson hoped Tanner still had that scotch from Scotland because, god, he needed a drink.

They drove in silence to his penthouse, the city lights casting shadows across Kinsley's face. When they arrived, he escorted her upstairs, giving her a brief tour that ended in his living room.

"Make yourself comfortable," he said, setting the food containers on the kitchen counter. "There's a bar in there if you want something to drink." He showed her the wet bar, half tempted to grab a bottle of brandy for the shitstorm he was about to walk into.

Kinsley stood in the center of his living room, looking both out of place and strangely right in his space. "I hope everything's okay with work."

The concern in her voice made something in his chest constrict. "It will be," he assured her, already heading for the door. "I'll be back as soon as I can."

Outside in the hallway, Carson finally responded to the group chat.

> On my way. How bad is it?

Benedict's response was immediate.

> Where the FUCK have you been? It's Richard Ashford's ghost coming back to haunt us. Someone's releasing documents.

Shit.

CHAPTER SEVEN

KINSLEY

Carson's penthouse occupied the top floor of a glass tower overlooking Central Park. It felt empty without him there though, more like a modern minimalist office than a home.

Kinsley wandered through the apartment, her heels clicking on the polished concrete floors. A massive sectional sofa in charcoal gray dominated the living room, facing a sleek fireplace and a TV that would make a sports bar jealous. The kitchen was a dream of stainless steel and white marble. It wasn't until she walked into his bedroom that it started to look like someone might live there. Personal touches scattered throughout drew Kinsley's attention.

She paused at a set of silver-framed photos on a shelf. One showed Carson with a blonde woman, their heads thrown back in laughter. The woman was beautiful, her blue eyes sparkling as she looked at Carson. Kinsley wondered who she was, a pang of jealousy tugging at her chest. Another photo showed Carson and Paisley as kids, grinning with ice cream cones in hand. Carson looked so carefree, so happy. So unlike the controlled, intense man she knew now.

Smiling, Kinsley set the photo down and continued farther into Carson's bedroom. A massive king-size bed sat in the middle with black and grey bedding. She was tempted to sit down, or even lie down, but the sheets and blankets didn't have a single wrinkle, and with another moment of hesitation, she moved onto his closet. Suits lined the walls, organized by color. In a row, his shoes sat polished and neatly arranged. She couldn't resist running her fingers along the sleeves of his suits. On a whim, she dropped her dress to the floor and pulled out one of his dress shirts, buttoning it up until the crisp white cotton fell halfway down her thighs. She knew it would drive him wild, and the thought sent a thrill through her.

Maybe then she'd get an up close view of the large bed.

And his large dick.

Her stomach dipped and she smirked. She'd almost had him finishing under the table at the restaurant, and would've if his damn phone hadn't interrupted him.

Back in the living room, she poured herself a glass of wine from the wet bar and chose a book from the shelves lining one wall. The titles were mostly boring. Nothing like the steamy smut she'd had in her apartment. The topics on his much neater bookshelf ranged from business strategy to true crime to the classics. Biting her lip, she sighed and selected a well-worn copy of "Pride and Prejudice," taking it and the wine to the couch. Kinsley curled up, tucking her feet under her.

The wine, the comfortable couch, and the familiar story combined to make Kinsley's eyelids heavy. She fought it at first, determined to stay awake until Carson returned. But the warmth of the fireplace and the soft hum of the city outside the windows lulled her into a sense of security. Her eyes fluttered closed, the book resting open on her chest.

She wasn't sure how much time had passed when Carson let himself into the apartment.

Kinsley woke to the soft brush of fingertips along her collarbone, tracing the open neckline of the dress shirt she wore. Her eyes fluttered. Carson crouched beside the couch, his steel-gray eyes locked onto hers. He'd ditched his jacket and tie, the top buttons of his shirt undone, revealing a hint of tanned skin.

"You're home," she murmured, stretching languidly. The shirt rode up her thighs, and Carson's gaze flicked down, then back up, a smirk playing on his lips.

"I am," he replied, his voice a low rumble. "Looks like you made yourself comfortable like I suggested."

She smirked, raising an eyebrow. "You like?"

"I love." He ran his thumb along the edge of the collar, his other finger dancing across her skin. However, the closer she looked at him, the more she noticed the dark circles under his eyes.

Kinsley sat up, the book tumbling to the floor. He picked it up, closing it and placing it on the glass coffee table beside him.

"Did you fix the crisis at work?"

Carson shrugged, his fingers now tracing the edge of the shirt, grazing the swell of her breasts. "It'll work itself out. Nothing to worry about."

Kinsley raised an eyebrow. "A little while ago, you were rushing out like your office building was on fire."

"No offense, sweetheart." He leaned in, his lips brushing her ear. "I'd rather talk about how much I love seeing you in my shirt. Or rather, how much I'd rather see what you're hiding beneath it."

His breath was hot on her neck, sending shivers down her spine. The heat of his body enveloped her along with the scent of his cologne.

"Is that so?" she managed to say, her voice barely above a whisper.

Carson nodded, his nose nuzzling her neck. "You have no idea what you do to me." His hand cupped her jaw, turning her face towards him. His breath mingling with hers. "You drive me crazy," he murmured before capturing her mouth in a searing kiss.

Kinsley melted into him, her hands gripping his shirt, pulling him closer. Carson's lips moved over hers. Damn, he knew exactly what he was doing. He bit at her lower lip, his tongue teasing, demanding entry. She eagerly complied. He tasted like mint, and she moaned into his mouth. Carson's hands roamed her body, slipping under the shirt, caressing her bare skin.

He pulled back slightly, his lips trailing down her neck, his large hands cupping her breasts. "Do you know how hard it makes me, seeing you like this?" he growled, his thumbs circling her nipples through the thin fabric of her bra.

Kinsley gasped, arching into his touch. "Show me," she challenged, her voice breathy.

Carson chuckled darkly. "Alright." He pushed her back against the couch, his body covering hers as he climbed on top. His lips found hers again, hungry and demanding. Kinsley moaned, her hands tugging at his clothes, desperate to feel his skin.

He broke the kiss, kneeling up to swiftly unbutton his shirt. Kinsley watched, her breath hitching as he revealed his muscled chest, a smattering of dark hair leading down to his lean abs. She reached out, her fingers tracing the lines of his muscles, the warmth of his skin.

God, he was perfect. Like a hero in the Greek myths.

Carson caught her wrist, bringing her hand to his lips. He kissed her palm, then her wrist, his tongue flicking out to taste her pulse point. "You're not the only one who's been going crazy, Kinsley," he said, his voice rough. "I've been thinking about this all day. About you. How much I am going to make you scream my name for all the city to hear."

Kinsley's stomach flipped, her body aching. Carson released her wrist, his hands going to the buttons of the shirt she wore. He undid them slowly, his eyes never leaving hers. He left a trail of kisses every place he exposed, from her chest all the way down to the edge of her underwear. When he stopped there, though, she whimpered a complaint.

"You're so beautiful," he murmured, pushing the shirt off her shoulders. "And I'm going to make you feel so fucking good."

He pulled her forward by the back of the neck, his mouth claimed hers as he unclasped her bra with his free hand. Her breasts spilled free. Carson's eyes darkened, his breath hitching. "Fuck, Kinsley," he growled, his hands cupping her breasts, his thumbs circling her nipples. "Such perfect tits," he murmured against her skin before he sucked one nipple in his mouth. He released it, looking up to meet her gaze. "Made to be sucked and fucked."

Kinsley arched into him, a moan escaping her lips. Carson's tongue lavished her nipples, his teeth gently nipping. Kinsley's hands gripped his hair. Trapped beneath him, her body writhed.

Carson's hand trailed down her skin, slipping under the waistband of her panties. His fingers found her wet and ready, a low groan rumbling from his chest. "Wet again for me, sweetheart?" His fingers stroked her. "What a good, fucking girl."

Kinsley gasped, her hips bucking against his hand. "Carson," she moaned, her hands gripping his shoulders.

He lifted his head, his eyes locking onto hers. "Beg," he said, his voice rough. "Say my name. Scream it." His slipped a finger inside her, his thumb circling her clit.

"Carson! Fuck!"

Kinsley's back arched as Carson's finger delved deeper, stroking her and curling in a way that left her gasping. One finger became two, stretching her. Filling her. Yet never quite enough to push her over the edge. She clung to him, her nails digging into his shoulders, her breath coming in ragged pants.

"Please," her voice came out a whimper. Her body was on fire, every nerve ending sparking. She was so close, teetering on the precipice of release, only to have him pull back again and again.

Carson's dark eyes watched her. There was a satisfaction in his gaze, a smugness that only fueled her frustration. "Come on Kinsley, beg," he demanded, his voice a low rumble. His thumb circled her clit, pressing hard enough to keep her spiraling, yet not hard or fast enough to push her over.

"Please," she begged, her voice barely above a whisper. Her hips bucked against his hand, seeking more friction, more pressure, more anything. Every time he pulled away just enough to deny her. "Fucking please, Carson."

He leaned in, his lips brushing her ear. "Please what?" His fingers slowed, almost to a stop, driving her mad.

"Please make me come." She dug her nails into his biceps hard enough to make him hiss. But he did not relent, even when her voice trembled. "Please, I need... I need..."

Carson pulled his fingers from her, bringing them to his mouth to lick clean. A wicked smirk crossed his lips. "I know what you need." He stood up, leaving her sprawled on the couch, a whimpering mess of need and frustration. "Jump," he commanded, holding out his hands.

Kinsley didn't hesitate. She launched herself at him, her legs wrapping around his waist, her arms around his neck. Carson caught her, his hands gripping her ass, pulling her tight against him. Their mouths collided again. She decided to take her frustration out on his lips, biting and nipping and bruising as his hand fisted the back of her hair and pulled her somehow closer.

He carried her through the apartment. She'd explored long enough to know exactly where he was headed. Finally. That fucking bed had been calling to her since the moment he'd woken her.

When they reached the bedroom, Carson dropped her onto the bed. She bounced, her breath hitching as she watched him, the place between her legs still throbbing and aching.

Carson didn't make her wait long. He spread her thighs wide, his eyes locked onto hers as he lowered down to his knees, his head hovering right above her center. The first touch of his tongue on her sensitive flesh had her crying out, her hips bucking off the bed. He licked and sucked, his fingers joining in, pushing her higher and higher until she was a writhing, moaning mess.

She broke and stars surrounded her. She screamed his name, her body tensing as the orgasm hit her.

But Carson didn't stop. Didn't slow down. He rode out her climax, pressing her hips down with a bruising grip. She writhed against him, trembling and swearing. His tongue and fingers working in tandem, wringing every last drop of pleasure from her.

When she finally came down, her body limp and sated, Carson rose. His eyes never left hers as he shed his pants and boxers, revealing the hard length of him. Fuck, he was just as big as she remembered. Kinsley's breath caught in her throat, her body already stirring with renewed desire.

Without a word, he flipped her roughly onto her hands and knees. A gasp escaped her lips, her heart pounding in her chest.

"Last chance, Kinsley," he growled, his voice a low rumble. "I don't do gentle. I fuck hard, and I fuck rough. If you can't handle that, tell me now."

Kinsley swallowed hard, her body trembling from her first orgasm. She looked back at him, her eyes meeting his steely gaze. "I can handle it," she said, her voice steady.

A smirk played on Carson's lips. "Good girl," he murmured, his hand trailing through her folds, gathering the moisture there and trailing it down her spine, sending shivers through her. "But I need to know, are you on birth control? Are you clean?"

Kinsley nodded, her breath hitching as his hand reached the curve of her ass. "Yes, and yes. You?"

"Clean as a whistle," he confirmed, his hand squeezing her ass cheek hard enough to make her yelp. He slapped it. "Let me make this clear, Kinsley. I'm going to fuck you raw. I'm going to fill you with my cum until it's dripping down your thighs. Understood?"

"Yes," she breathed, her voice barely above a whisper. "Please, Carson. Just do it already."

A dark chuckle escaped his lips. "With pleasure," he growled.

He gripped her hips, his fingers digging into her soft flesh. Kinsley braced herself, her heart pounding in her chest. The head of his cock pushed at her entrance. He didn't ease in gently once he was lined up. With one swift thrust, he buried himself deep inside her.

Kinsley cried out, her body stretching to accommodate him. He was big, filling her completely. Pain mixed with pleasure, her body on fire. God, it burned, but in a way that she would've happily burned forever. Carson stilled for a moment, his breath ragged.

"Fuck, you're tight," he growled, his fingers gripping her hips tighter. "Even with me finger fucking you. God, you're perfect."

Kinsley panted, her body adjusting to his size. Something in her heated at his praise. "More," she begged, her voice breathy. "Please, Carson. More."

He didn't need more encouragement. Carson pulled back, only to slam back into her, his hips snapping forward to hit her ass every time. Kinsley gripped the sheets, her knuckles white as she held on, her body rocking with each thrust.

Carson's hands roamed her body, gripping her ass, her hips, her breasts. He leaned over her, his body covering hers as he fucked her hard. The angle had him going deeper than she'd ever taken any man, and she whimpered and sobbed into the sheets. His breath was hot on her neck, his teeth nipping at her shoulder.

"You feel so fucking good," he growled, his voice rough. "Your pussy is perfect, Kinsley. Made for me. Fucking made for me."

Kinsley moaned, her body on fire. Each thrust sent waves of pleasure coursing through her. Another orgasm started to build, her body tensing.

"My little whore," he murmured, his lips against her ear. "You like being fucked like this. Used. Controlled." He slapped her on the ass cheek and she whimpered.

Her body pushed back against him as a response, taking him deeper. Carson's thrusts grew harder, and he reached around, gripping her by the throat. Fuck, that drove her closer. His hand snaked around to rub her clit. He moved in tight circles, and she moaned at the touch.

"Come for me, Kinsley," he commanded, his voice a low rumble. "Let me feel you come all over my cock."

Kinsley gasped, her body trembling. She was so close, teetering on the edge. Carson tightened his grip on her throat, and she gasped, her mind already beginning to fracture.

"Come on, Kinsley," he growled, his voice rough as he slapped her ass again. "Be a good girl and come for me."

With a cry, Kinsley came undone. Her body tensed, her orgasm crashing over her in waves. She screamed his name, her body convulsing around him. Carson rode out her orgasm, his thrusts growing erratic.

"Fuck, Kinsley, fuck," he growled, his body tensing. With a final thrust, he came, his cock pulsing inside her. Heat from his release filled her and she struggled to breathe.

They stayed like that for a moment, their bodies joined, their breaths ragged. Carson's body covered hers, his arms wrapped around her, holding her close. His heart pounded against her back.

Slowly, Carson pulled out. Kinsley collapsed onto the bed, her body spent, her limbs heavy. She watched as Carson stood, his body glistening with sweat. He looked down at her, his eyes dark, a satisfied smirk playing on his lips.

"Stay there," he commanded, his voice rough. "I'll be right back."

Kinsley didn't move, her body too sated to do anything but lie there. She watched as Carson walked to the bathroom, his muscled ass on full display. She heard the sound of running water, and a moment later, Carson returned, a warm washcloth in his hand.

He climbed onto the bed, his body straddling hers. Gently, he cleaned her, his touch surprisingly tender. Kinsley watched him, her heart fluttering in her chest. This man, who had just fucked her rough and raw, was now taking care of her. But, she supposed, that's what he'd been doing since she'd signed her life away to him.

When he was done, he tossed the washcloth aside and settled next to her. He pulled her into his arms, her back pressed against his chest. She snuggled into him, a content sigh escaping her lips.

"You were better than I could've ever imagine," Carson murmured, his voice soft.

Kinsley beamed. "I've never been fucked like that," she admitted.

Carson chuckled, his arms tightening around her. "Good," he said, his voice rough. "Because I'm not done with you yet."

Kinsley's pulse spiked. "Is that so?" she said, her voice teasing.

Carson's hand trailed down her body, his fingers finding her sensitive flesh. "Oh, yes," he growled, his voice a low rumble. "I'm going to fuck you again, Kinsley. And again. Until you can't walk straight. Until you're screaming my name so loud, the whole building knows who you belong to."

Kinsley moaned, her body arching into his touch. "And who do I belong to?" she said, her voice breathy.

Carson's fingers slipped between her legs, his thumb circling her tender clit. "Me, Kinsley," he growled, his voice rough. "You belong to me."

Kinsley moaned, her body on fire. She belonged to him. Carson Fucking Crest owned her. All of her.

CHAPTER EIGHT

KINSLEY

KINSLEY STIRRED AWAKE, HER BODY DELICIOUSLY SORE from the night before. She stretched, the silk sheets sliding against her skin. Blinking slowly, she opened her eyes and took in the room with the morning light streaming through the large floor to ceiling windows. She hadn't really noticed them the night before, too busy climaxing eleven—wait, was it twelve?—times.

The sound of running water drew her attention to the en suite bathroom, where steam billowed from the slightly ajar door. She pictured Carson under the spray, water cascading down the body she'd worshipped the night before. The mere thought sent a shiver of desire through her, and she was tempted to join him. Her body ached for more. It also just ached. But there were other things that she could think of that wouldn't bother her sensitive pussy. Heat pooled in her stomach as she threw back the sheets.

She made the mistake of reaching for her phone first, though. The screen exploded with hundreds of alerts, all time stamped within the last hour. But these weren't the glowing profiles of Carson's generosity or Crest Strategies' innovative approach to reputation rehabilitation.

Her stomach clenched with familiar dread. Not again. Please, not again.

She opened her notifications with trembling fingers, and her world tilted sideways. Someone had leaked security footage from Carson's building. Kinsley squinted against the bright screen, her heart pounding as she scrolled through the notifications. Her eyes widened in horror at the headlines splashed across various gossip sites.

Kinsley's grip on the phone tightened. Bile rose in her throat as she saw the explicit images—blurred but unmistakably her and Carson—splashed across the screen. Taken through the very windows she now sat naked beside. She gripped the sheets, pulling them up to cover herself.

"No," she whispered, her breath hitching as she read the captions. The articles were brutal, painting her as a seductress who slept her way back into the spotlight. The comments section was a cesspool of hate, with people calling her every derogatory name under the sun. But it was the threats, the legitimate, terrifying threats, that sent a shiver of fear down her spine.

The phone slipped from her grasp, clattering onto the floor. Hot tears welled in her eyes, blurring her vision. She hugged her knees to her chest around the sheets, feeling exposed and vulnerable. The sobs came suddenly, wracking her body as she let the fear and humiliation consume her.

The bathroom door creaked open, and Carson stepped out, a towel slung low around his hips. His hair was damp, water droplets clinging to his broad shoulders. He paused, his gaze flicking from her tear-streaked face to the phone lying face up on the floor.

"Kinsley?" His voice was sharp. He crossed the room in a few quick strides, sitting kneeling on the floor in front of her. "What happened? What's wrong?"

She couldn't speak, couldn't find the words to explain the horror unfolding on her screen. Instead, she pointed a shaky finger at the phone, her body trembling with sobs.

Carson picked up the device, his brows furrowing as he read. His jaw tightened. A muscle ticked in his cheek as he scrolled through the articles.

Kinsley knew what he was seeing.

"Kinsley Ellis Seduces Her Way Back into the Limelight."

"She's literally fucking her way back to relevance"

"Poor Carson Crest getting manipulated by this desperate whore"

"All that good PR about second chances—turns out she was just spreading her legs for it"

"Crest Strategies about to learn what happens when you trust a fake bitch"

"Someone should teach her a lesson she won't forget."

"She deserves to be thrown off a bridge for what she's done."

"I hope she chokes on her own lies."

"Shit," Carson muttered, his voice doing nothing to hide his anger. He glanced up at her, his eyes softening with something that looked almost like tenderness. "Kinsley, I don't know how this happened, but it is not your fault."

She let out a shaky laugh, swiping at her tears with the back of her hand. "I've ruined this. You're being dragged through hell because of me. Why does this keep happening?"

Carson's expression darkened. He tossed the phone aside and cupped her face in his hands, forcing her to meet his gaze. "Listen to me, sweetheart. Do not be worried about me. We will fix this. I will find out who is responsible and they will pay." He tucked a strand of curly hair behind her ear and then brushed her tears from her cheeks. "We were in my private apartment, behind closed doors. Someone invaded our privacy. They're the ones at fault, not you."

Kinsley leaned into his hands, drawing strength from his words. "But the threats, Carson. They're serious. People want to hurt me."

"What threats?" His eyes flashed with something dark, and he reached for the phone. Within seconds, a fierce protectiveness crossed his face. "Fuck this. Fuck them. No one is going to hurt you, Kinsley. I promise you that. I'll find out who did this, and I'll make them pay."

She believed him. She trusted Carson would keep her safe.

He hadn't given her a reason not to.

God, how was she falling for this man as her world fell apart?

Carson pulled her into his arms, holding her tightly against his bare chest. His comforting heart beat soothed her frayed nerves. His fingers tangled in her hair, stroking gently as he murmured reassurances into her ear.

"I'll get you through this. I won't let anyone hurt you. I protect what's mine, Kinsley. And you're mine."

She clung to him, her tears subsiding as she absorbed his strength. It felt good to be held, to be protected. It felt right.

"Come on," he said, pulling back. "Let's get you cleaned up from last night, and then we'll discuss what to do about all of this." He helped her up, letting her take the sheet with her. He closed the blinds on the windows, sending the room into darkness until he flipped on the lights. "Go get in the shower. I'm going to go make some phone calls and then I'll join you."

Kinsley nodded, not bothering to point out that he didn't have to join her. No. She wanted him to. She didn't want to be alone with her thoughts.

Still though, she obeyed and stepped into the shower. The hot water cascaded over her body. She tipped her head back, letting the spray soak her hair, washing away the remnants of last night. Her muscles ached, but the hot water helped relax them bit by bit. She reached for Carson's shampoo, inhaling the scent of sandalwood and citrus. It likely would dry out her curls, but she didn't have much of an option since her shampoo was—she paused before squirting the shampoo into her hand. Another bottle sat beside it, smaller, but familiar.

It was her favorite.

Kinsley let out a small giggle, replacing Carson's shampoo and taking the small bottle he'd clearly gotten for her.

When had he done that?

The grin didn't leave her lips as Kinsley lathered her hair. The smell was familiar and helped to ground her.

That is, until strong hands gripped her hips, making her jump. She glanced over her shoulder to see Carson, naked and stepping under the spray with her. Water droplets clung to his lashes, his gaze dark.

She leaned back against him, his erection pressing into her lower back.

"Hey," she whispered, her voice barely audible over the sound of the water.

He didn't respond with words. Instead, he leaned down, capturing her lips in a fierce kiss. His hands roamed her body, cupping her breasts, teasing her nipples until she moaned into his mouth. His cock hardened more against her, and despite the soreness between her legs, she wanted him again. She needed this. Needed him to distract her from the chaos outside.

Carson's mouth moved to her neck, kissing and biting gently as his hands explored every inch of her skin. She appreciated how her body fit perfectly against his. She reached back, wrapping her hand around him. He groaned, thrusting into her grip.

"Turn," he growled, his voice low and dangerous. "I need to be inside you."

She turned to face him, her back pressing against the cool tiles of the shower wall. Carson captured her mouth again, his kiss hungry and demanding. He lifted her, wrapping her legs around his waist, and the tip of his cock nudged at her entrance. She winced as he pushed inside, her core still sensitive.

Carson paused, concern flashing in his eyes. "Does it hurt?" he asked, his voice gentler than she'd expected.

She bit her lip, nodding. "A little," she admitted. "But don't stop."

He studied her for a moment, then nodded. "You're in control," he said, his voice rough. "Take what you need, sweetheart."

She wrapped her arms around his neck, using her leverage to lower herself onto him. She gasped as he filled her, the sensation a mix of pleasure and pain. Carson held her tightly, his body tense with restraint as she began to move, setting the pace.

She rode him slowly at first, her body adjusting to the invasion. Carson's grip on her tightened, his fingers digging into her flesh as he fought to resist control. She could see the effort it took, could see the muscles in his jaw ticking as he let her take the lead.

But even as she set the pace, Carson still managed to take

charge. His hips thrust up to meet hers, his cock hitting that spot deep inside her that made her spiral higher. Soon, she gave up control, needing him to take her as he had before. As soon as she begged him to fuck her, a switch flipped. He was rough, thrusting deep and pinning her between him and the wall. She clung to him, her nails digging into his shoulders as she met his thrusts.

Steam rose around them, cocooning them in a world of their own. There was no scandal, no threats. Just the two of them, lost in the primal rhythm of their bodies.

Kinsley's breath hitched as Carson hit a particularly sensitive spot. He must've noticed because he adjusted his angle to hit it again and again and again. He pumped into her. She clawed at his back, needing him closer.

"Carson, I—" Pleasure coiled tightly in her belly, her orgasm building and stealing her ability to form words. Carson's body started tensing too, his cock swelling inside her. He was close.

She leaned forward, capturing his mouth in a fierce kiss. "Don't stop," she gasped against his lips. "Don't you dare stop."

Carson growled, his hips moving faster, his thrusts becoming more urgent. Messy. He was close, so close, and she wanted to feel him come undone inside her.

Her own orgasm hit her without her expecting it and her scream died in her throat, her body tightening around him. She gasped, convulsing. Her nails dug into his skin as waves of pleasure crashed over her. Carson thrust into her once, twice more, before finding his own release. He shouted her name mixed in with profanity, his body shuddering as he came inside her.

Their breaths came in ragged gasps. Then, slowly, Carson lowered her to the ground, his cock slipping out of her. She winced.

Carson noticed, his eyes softening with concern. "Are you okay?" he asked, his voice gentle.

She nodded, offering him a small smile. "I'm better," she said. "Better thanks to you."

He returned her smile, then reached for the soap. "We should finish in here," he said, his voice returning to its usual commanding tone.

"I thought we just did."

Carson's genuine laugh was beautiful, and not something Kinsley thought she'd ever heard before. It brought a smile to her lips as he stepped closer.

"We did." He kissed her once before dropping to his knees with the soap, and fuck if she wasn't ready to go for shower sex, round two.

Instead, she let him wash her, his hands gentle as they ran over her body. He shampooed her hair again because she didn't bother to remind him that she'd already done it once. Her hair would recover. Besides, his fingers massaging her scalp nearly had her dropping to her knees for him. Kinsley purred with contentment.

When they were both clean, Carson turned off the water and stepped out of the shower. He grabbed a towel, wrapping it around his waist before grabbing another for her. He held it open, inviting her into his embrace. She stepped into it, letting him wrap the towel around her, cocooning her in warmth and his scent.

"Come on," he said, leading her out of the bathroom.

She followed him, her body still tingling. Kinsley was content to stay in this bubble with Carson, to let him take care of her. She didn't have any desire to leave his penthouse as long as he fed her.

And fucked her.

As they stepped into the bedroom, the sound of Carson's phone ringing filled the air. He glanced at the screen, his expression turning serious. "I need to take this," he said, pressing a kiss to her forehead. "I'll be right back."

She nodded, watching as he stepped out of the room, the phone pressed to his ear. She took a deep breath. She couldn't hide in this bubble forever.

CHAPTER NINE

CARSON

WATCHING KINSLEY STAND NAKED IN HIS CLOSET WHILE his phone exploded with notifications about their leaked footage made Carson want to burn the world down. Something inside him had broken, and Kinsley had been the one to wield the sledge hammer.

Carson's grip on his phone tightened as he paced the bedroom. His voice was dangerously low, a growl meant to contain the rage that threatened to explode.

"I don't give a damn about protocol, Ben. I want to know who took those photos and how they got distributed to every fucking tabloid in three hours." He glanced at Kinsley, who was rifling through the bags of designer clothes he'd had delivered. Her hands trembled as she examined a cashmere sweater.

"We're working on it," Benedict replied, his usual calm sounding strained. "Penn's trying to trace the source, but whoever did this covered their tracks exceptionally well."

"Tell him to try harder," Carson hissed, turning away from Kinsley. "This isn't some random paparazzi shot. Someone was watching us and taking fucking pictures."

"That's not our only problem," Benedict said. "The Ashford case documents that leaked yesterday—"

"I don't care about Ashford right now." The moment the words left his mouth, Carson realized how true they were. Four and a half years of obsession with destroying Kinsley Ellis had evaporated overnight, replaced by an overwhelming need to protect her.

Benedict's phone beeped over the line.

"Who was that?"

The resounding silence spoke volumes.

"Benedict, what aren't you telling me?" Carson demanded.

"I sent Jenna and the security team to Kinsley's apartment. That was Tanner giving me an update. Cars, Kinsley's apartment was broken into. It's completely destroyed."

Ice cut through Carson's veins. "What do you mean 'destroyed'?"

"Furniture slashed, walls damaged, personal items smashed. It looks personal, Carson. Not a random burglary."

Carson's gaze snapped to Kinsley, who was now watching him with concern in her eyes. He attempted a reassuring smile, but judging by the way her forehead creased, he'd failed miserably.

"Hold on," he said to Benedict, then muted the call. "Can I see your phone for a second?"

"Sure," she said, handing it over without hesitation.

Carson scrolled through her messages, finding the explicit and violent threats he'd seen before. They detailed what would happen when they found her at her apartment. His jaw clenched so tight he thought his teeth might crack.

He unmuted the call. "Benedict, she's received direct threats. Specific ones. About exactly this. I'm sending them to you now."

"Jesus," Benedict muttered, likely looking at the screenshots. "I'll forward these to Penn. We need to identify—"

"No, what we need is to lock this down now. I'm bringing Kinsley to the office. Get everyone in the conference room. We're handling this in person."

"Carson, with the media circling after the Ashford leak—"

"I don't give a fuck about optics right now," Carson snapped. "Is Jenna back?"

"Yes."

"Have her ready with security outside the building. We'll be there in twenty."

He ended the call and turned to Kinsley, who stood clutching a silk blouse to her chest.

"What's happening?" she asked, that frown still on her pretty face.

Carson crossed the room and ran his hands down her arms. "Someone broke into your apartment."

Her eyes widened. "What? When? How bad is it?"

"It's bad," he said, deciding not to shield her from the truth. "But what matters is that you weren't there when it happened. We're going to my office. I have my entire team working to find out who's behind this."

"Someone's targeting us."

"Yes." Carson squeezed her arms. "But they're targeting the wrong people. Whoever's doing this doesn't know who they're dealing with."

Kinsley nodded, her shoulders straightening. "What should I wear?"

"Something comfortable but professional. There will likely be reporters outside, but we might be there a while."

While she dressed, Carson made calls, arranging for additional security measures and instructing his driver to bring the car to the private garage entrance. He watched Kinsley from the corner of his eye. The woman he'd spent years vilifying in his mind was showing more strength than he'd ever given her credit for.

When had everything changed? Was it when she'd told him about her parents turning their backs on her? Or when she'd looked into his eyes last night, vulnerable and trusting as she finished with him over and over again? Perhaps it was this morning, seeing raw fear in her eyes as her privacy was violated again.

The reason didn't matter. What mattered was that Carson Crest no longer saw Kinsley Ellis as his enemy.

But she was his.

His to protect.

"Ready?" he asked as she finished buttoning a navy blazer over a simple white top.

"As I'll ever be," she replied with a brittle smile.

During the tense and silent ride to Crest Strategies, Carson kept one hand on Kinsley's thigh, his other hand constantly checking for updates from his team. She leaned into him, and something protective and fierce roared to life inside him.

As their car approached the building, Carson swore under his breath. The sidewalk swarmed with reporters and photographers, a feeding frenzy of vultures waiting to tear at fresh meat.

"There are a lot of them," Kinsley whispered, shrinking back against the leather seat.

"Jenna and her team will get us through." He squeezed her hand. "Stay close to me. Don't respond to anything they say, no matter what it is."

When the car stopped, Carson's head of security, Jenna Briggs, opened the door herself, her tall frame blocking most of the cameras. Four other security personnel formed a tight perimeter around the car.

"Ready when you are, Mr. Crest," Jenna said, her professional expression blank despite the chaos.

Carson stepped out first, then turned to help Kinsley. The moment she emerged, the crowd erupted.

"Kinsley! How does it feel to be exposed again?"

"Mr. Crest! Is this relationship just a publicity stunt?"

"Are you concerned about the Ashford documents?"

"Kinsley! Did you leak the photos yourself?"

Carson pulled Kinsley against his side, using his body as a shield. She trembled against him and Carson tightened his grip, leaning down to speak directly into her ear.

"Ignore them. They don't exist. Be a good girl and just walk."

Jenna led the way, physically pushing back reporters who got too close. Camera flashes exploded around them like artillery fire. Carson kept his eyes forward. He'd had plenty of years practicing his mask of cold indifference. It hid the fury building inside him. One reporter lunged forward, microphone extended like a weapon, and Carson moved without thinking, placing himself between the man and Kinsley.

"Back up," he growled, his voice cutting through the crowd.

The reporter faltered, Carson's expression making him step back. They continued their advance toward the building's entrance, where two more security guards held the doors open.

Once inside the lobby, the sudden silence was almost disorienting. Kinsley released a shaky breath.

"You okay?" Carson asked, examining her face.

She nodded. "That was... intense."

"Ms. Ellis, Mr. Crest," Jenna said, "the others are waiting in the main conference room. I've secured the entire floor."

"Thank you, Jenna," Carson replied. "Double the security presence throughout the building. No one gets in without direct authorization from me."

"Already done, sir."

The elevator ride to the top floor was silent. Carson watched Kinsley's reflection in the polished doors, noting how she squared her shoulders and lifted her chin just before they opened. Preparing for battle.

The conference room doors were closed when they approached. Carson paused, turning to Kinsley.

"These men are the best at what they do," he said quietly. "They're also protective and probably angry right now. Not at you," he added quickly. "At the situation."

"Should I be scared of them?" she asked with a small attempt at humor.

"No. But they might be a lot to handle all at once."

She nodded. "I can handle it."

Carson pushed open the doors to find his four partners standing around the conference table. Benedict leaned over Penn's shoulder, his usual perfect composure fraying at the edges. Penn's fingers flew across three different keyboards, his face illuminated by multiple screens. Tanner paced near the windows, a phone to his ear while James stood with his arms crossed, his expression grim.

All four men looked up as Carson and Kinsley entered.

"Gentlemen," Carson said, guiding Kinsley forward with a hand at the small of her back. "I believe you all know Kinsley Ellis."

Benedict was the first to move, stepping forward to offer his hand. "Ms. Ellis. I wish we were meeting under better circumstances."

"Kinsley, please," she replied, shaking his hand. "And thank you for helping."

The others introduced themselves with varying degrees of formality. Tanner merely nodded. Penn gave an awkward half-wave with one hand without stopping his typing with the other. James offered a tight smile and a firm handshake.

"What do we know?" Carson asked, pulling out a chair for Kinsley before taking his own.

"Not enough," Tanner said, blunt as always. "Briggs said the apartment break-in was professional. No fingerprints, no DNA, security cameras disabled."

"You mean my apartment?" Kinsley asked, and Tanner nodded, but Penn answered.

"Yes. And the photo leak is even more concerning," Penn added, swiveling one of his screens to show them a complex web of data points. "Whoever did this used a sophisticated distribution algorithm. Multiple anonymous accounts activated simultaneously across different platforms, all with pre-loaded content. By the time the first image was flagged, it had already been copied and reshared thousands of times."

"The timing isn't coincidental," Benedict said, his ice-blue eyes fixed on Carson. "This happened twelve hours after the Ashford documents leaked."

Kinsley stiffened beside him. "What documents?"

The four men exchanged glances, and Carson realized he'd kept her in the dark about a crucial piece of information.

"Three years ago, Crest Strategies was involved in a case concerning a corrupt man named Richard Ashford," he explained, choosing his words carefully. "Yesterday, confidential documents about that case were leaked to several news outlets."

"And you think it's connected to what's happening to me?" Kinsley asked.

"It's a possibility. But, we believe it's less about you, Ms. Ellis, and more about him," James said, nodding towards Carson. "Two major attacks on Crest's reputation within twenty-four hours is unlikely to be coincidence."

"Which means this isn't about the photos or your apartment," Benedict said, turning to Kinsley. "Someone is using you to get to Carson, to hurt Crest Strategies."

Her eyes widened. "I'm collateral damage."

Carson rubbed a hand over his face, leaning forward. When had control slipped from his fingers this badly?

"I'm sorry, Kinsley," Carson said with a sigh.

She glanced at him, her eyes wide. "It's not your fault. Benedict just said—"

"It *is* my fault." Carson sank back into his chair, and thanked Tanner when he slid him a glass of Scotch. "I brought you into my world, and now it'll burn you down too."

"Fuck that," Kinsley said, shaking her head. Across the table, Penn raised an eyebrow and a ghost of a smile crossed over Tanner's face. "My world was already burning down when you saved me from the flames."

Carson felt sick. The only reason her world had burned was because he covered it in gasoline and struck the match.

God, she could never find out.

"As...touching as that is," Tanner said, his nose wrinkling and his stone mask back in place, "Finding who's behind this is our top priority."

"All due respect," Benedict interrupted, "the Ashford leak contains potentially criminal allegations. That has to be our primary concern."

"I don't give a damn about Ashford right now," Carson snapped. "Kinsley is receiving direct threats. Her home was invaded. She's not safe right now. She is our client. She is our priority. As CEO of Crest Strategies, I say to hell with the rest."

All four men stared at him, varying degrees of shock on their faces.

Carson realized he'd never spoken to them like this before. While yes, the business held his last name, they'd always been a team. He'd never once pulled the CEO card and let personal concerns override business interests.

"Carson," Benedict said carefully, "may I speak with you privately for a moment?"

"Anything you have to say can be said in front of her."

Benedict's jaw tightened. "Fine. I don't know when this became real for you," he said, gesturing between Carson and Kinsley, "But clearly you're compromised. Your judgment is clouded, and you're making decisions based on emotion rather than strategy."

"Fuck you. My judgment is perfectly clear," Carson replied, slamming the empty Scotch glass on the table. "Someone is targeting a civilian to get to us. That makes it our responsibility to protect her."

"So this has nothing to do with the two of you fucking?" Tanner asked, and Carson shot to his feet.

"Watch your goddamn mouth, Whitney, or I'll—"

"You'll what?" Tanner responded, crossing the room in two long strides. He had a good three inches on Carson and had been trained in the military. If a fight broke out, it would not be pretty.

"Would you two shut up and sit down?" James shouted, stepping between them and pushing them apart. "You're acting like children and it's getting us no where."

"We're not disagreeing about protecting Ms. Ellis," Penn interjected. "But we need to address both threats simultaneously."

Carson was about to argue when Kinsley placed her hand on his arm. He didn't know when she'd stood up, but she was there, pulling him back to his chair. "Carson, they're right. If this is connected to your company, you can't ignore that part."

He stared at her, surprised by her calm rationality in the face of everything happening.

"Fine." He pinched the bridge of his nose. "What do you suggest?" he asked, addressing all of them.

"Break into teams," Benedict said immediately. "I'll speak with Briggs and handle the threat to Ms. Ellis's security. Penn focuses on tracking down whoever leaked the photos and broke into her apartment. Tanner and James deal with the Ashford situation."

"And me?" Carson asked.

"You're too close to both situations," Benedict said. "You need to step back and let us handle this."

Carson's laugh was sharp. "That's not happening."

"Then at least recognize your bias," Benedict pressed. "You're not thinking clearly where Kinsley is concerned."

Carson felt Kinsley's eyes on him but couldn't bring himself to meet her gaze. "Fine. We split into teams as Ben suggested. But I'm staying with Kinsley."

Benedict opened his mouth to object, then closed it, resignation crossing his features. "Fine."

"Where will she stay?" Penn asked, finally looking up from his screens. "Her apartment isn't safe, and if someone got photos from your penthouse..."

"For now, we'll be in my office," Carson said. "Ben, have Jenna find us somewhere safe to go later."

"I'll arrange transportation," Benedict said, already pulling out his phone.

As the others began coordinating their efforts, Carson finally turned to Kinsley. "I am sorry," he said quietly. "This is my fault."

She studied him for a long moment. "We are both being played by someone. It's not your fault."

"Come on," he said, pulling her to her feet. "Let's go to my office."

CHAPTER TEN

KINSLEY

IF KINSLEY WAS BEING HONEST, SHE WAS DAMN SCARED. But she didn't dare tell Carson that. He already seemed distraught as he paced back and forth in his office. As soon as they'd entered the room, he'd shut all the blinds with a click of a button. At least there was some privacy.

She perched on Carson's desk, her attention tracking his striding from one end of the large room to the other. He was unraveling, his usual composure shattered by the morning's events. She'd never seen him like this, his steel-gray eyes stormy, his hair disheveled from running his hands through it one too many times. She tried to reassure him, telling him they'd figure it out, that it would be okay, but her words seemed to bounce off him, leaving no impact.

"Carson," she tried again, but he was already mid-rant, his voice a low growl as he detailed all the ways he was going to destroy whoever was behind this. She sighed, watching him wear a path into the plush carpet.

An idea sparked in her mind. A way she might be able to help him calm down. She slid off the desk, her bare feet sinking into the carpet as she walked to the door and clicked the lock into place.

Carson paused, his eyes narrowing as he watched her kneel in the middle of the room, right in the path of his pacing. "What are you doing?"

She stared up at him with a smile on her lips. "Giving you something else to think about," she said, her voice steady despite the butterflies in her stomach.

He raised an eyebrow, his gaze darkening as he seemed to realize her intent. "And what makes you think I want that right now?" he challenged, but the flicker of interest in his eyes didn't escape her attention.

"Because," she said, her voice barely above a whisper, "I think you need it. I think you need to be in control of something right now. So control me."

He studied her for a moment, his jaw clenched, before he grabbed her chin, his thumb tracing her bottom lip. "Open," he commanded, and she complied, parting her lips. He stuck a long finger into her mouth and she lavished it with her tongue. When he pushed it farther, hitting the back of her throat, her eyes watered and she held back from gagging until she couldn't stand it. Carson's predatory smile sent a shiver through her. He pinched her cheeks, holding her mouth open as he spat, his eyes never leaving hers. "Take off my belt," he ordered, his voice rough.

Kinsley reached up, her fingers fumbling as she pulled the leather belt from his pants. He took it from her, his fingers brushing against hers, sending a shiver down her spine. "Now my pants," he commanded next.

Her fingers worked the button and zipper. The outline of his hard cock shown behind the thin layer of his boxers, and a surge of satisfaction filled her chest knowing she had done that to him.

"Take out my cock," he ordered, his voice a low growl.

She did as she was told, her fingers wrapping around his length. He was hot and hard in her hands, and she looked up at him, waiting for his next command. He didn't make her wait long. He grabbed her wrists, pulling them behind her back and wrapping the belt around them, securing them in place.

Carson grabbed her hair, his fingers tangling in her curls as he roughly pulled her head back. "Open your mouth," he commanded, his voice rough. She complied, her mouth open wide, her tongue ready for him.

"You *will* swallow."

He thrust into her mouth, his grip on her hair tightening. Carson was rough, his hips moving at a punishing pace, but she took it all, her tongue lavishing his dick, taking him as far back down her throat as she could. She gagged, her eyes watering, but she didn't stop, didn't pull back. She loved it, loved the feeling of him in her mouth, loved the taste of him, loved the rough, dirty words he was growling at her.

"That's it, sweetheart," he groaned, his hips moving faster. "Take it all. Take everything I give you."

She did, her mouth working him, her tongue teasing him. He was getting closer, his cock swelling in her mouth. He thrust one last time, hitting the back of her throat, making her gag again as he came, his hot cum shooting down her throat. He held her there, his cock buried in her mouth, his fingers tangled in her hair, until he was spent.

When he finally released her, she coughed, her throat raw, but she grinned up at him, her face covered in his essence. "Feel better?" she asked, her voice hoarse.

Carson looked at her, his gaze softening. He reached down, his thumb brushing against her cheek, wiping away a drop of cum. "Yes," he said. "Yes, I do." He pulled her up until she was standing, and bent down to kiss her. "Incredible, Kinsley. You are incredible, and I don't deserve you."

"I—"

His phone rang before Kinsley could tell him he was wrong and that they deserved each other. He apologized, quickly freeing her arms before zipping himself back up and answering the phone.

Kinsley wobbled to her feet, her knees shaky. She grabbed a tissue from his desk and cleaned herself up, her eyes never leaving him as he paced the length of the office again, phone pressed to his ear. His voice was low, too low for her to make out the words, but the tension in his shoulders spoke volumes.

She tossed the tissue into the trash can and was about to ask him if everything was okay when a text came in and he looked at it. The color drained from his face in an instant. His grip tightened on the phone. He looked like he'd seen a ghost.

Carson ended the call abruptly, his hand dropping to his side, the phone still clutched tightly in his fingers. He stared at the screen, his brow furrowed, his breath coming in short, sharp gasps.

"Carson?" Kinsley asked, her voice soft, tentative. "What's wrong?"

He looked up at her, and she recognized the fear there. "I... I have to go speak with Penn," he stammered, his voice barely above a whisper.

Kinsley took a step towards him, her hand reaching out to touch his arm. "Go where? What's happening?"

He flinched away from her touch, his gaze darting back to his phone. "I'm sorry, Kinsley. I can't... I can't explain right now. I have to go."

Before she could say another word, he was out the door, leaving her alone in the vast office. She stared at the closed door, her mind racing, her heart pounding in her chest. What the hell just happened?

She sank down into his desk chair, scanning the room, looking for any clue that could explain his sudden departure. His laptop was still open, his jacket still draped over the back of the chair, his coffee still steaming on the desk. Whatever it was, it must have been important. Important enough to make him leave without any explanation.

Kinsley sighed, running her hands through her hair. She couldn't just sit here and wait for him to come back. She needed answers. She needed to know what was going on. Kinsley reached for his laptop, her fingers brushing against the touchpad, bringing the screen to life.

She shouldn't be doing this. Invading Carson's privacy felt wrong, but she couldn't shake the look on his face before he'd rushed out. Something wasn't right.

"Just a quick peek," she whispered to herself, clicking on his email.

Nothing suspicious there. Just business correspondence, meeting invitations, and reports. She clicked through his folders, scanning for anything unusual. A folder labeled "Project Ellis" caught her eye. She clicked on it, expecting to find information about her image rehabilitation.

The air left her lungs.

Photos of her. Hundreds of them. Dating back years. Screenshots of her social media posts, surveillance photos of her entering buildings, sitting in cafes, shopping. Some taken with telephoto lenses from far away, others clearly from security cameras.

"What the hell?" she whispered, her heart hammering against her ribs.

She clicked on a document titled "Timeline." A detailed record of her movements, activities, and communications for the past four and a half years. Every post, every public appearance, every brand deal, all meticulously documented and analyzed.

Her hands shook as she scrolled through the document. This wasn't recent. This predated her cancellation by years. This predated her even knowing who Carson Crest was.

A subfolder caught her eye: "Project Emma."

With trembling fingers, she clicked on it. A series of documents appeared, detailing a systematic plan to destroy Kinsley's career, reputation, and ultimately her life. Step by step. Calculated.

The first document was dated four years ago.

Phase 1: Surveillance and Intelligence Gathering

Subject: Kinsley Ellis

Objective: Complete psychological profile, routine mapping, vulnerability assessment

She couldn't breathe. This wasn't happening. This couldn't be real.

She clicked on a more recent document labeled "Trigger Event."

A video file appeared. She recognized it immediately. The infamous 37-second clip that had started her downward spiral. The hot mic moment where she'd carelessly said her followers would buy anything she promoted. She remembered that day; she'd been exhausted, frustrated after a 14-hour shoot with a difficult brand manager. The words had slipped out, never meant for public consumption.

But according to this document, Carson had orchestrated its release. Had paid someone on her team to record it, edit it to remove context, and leak it strategically when it would do maximum damage.

"No," she whispered, tears blurring her vision. "No, no, no."

She clicked on another file: "Phase 2: Isolation Protocol."

Objective: Systematic removal of support systems

- Target key brand relationships (Complete)

- Compromise management team (Complete)

- Alienate close friends and family (Complete)

- Financial destabilization (Complete)

Everything, every terrible thing that had happened to her in the past months, had been orchestrated by Carson. The man who'd offered to save her. The man she'd trusted. The man she'd fallen for.

The man she'd just been on her knees for.

Bile rose in her throat. She barely made it to the trash can before retching, her body rejecting the horror of what she'd discovered.

When she straightened, wiping her mouth with the back of her hand, her eyes fell on one more folder on the laptop: "Emma Christensen."

With shaking hands, she clicked on it.

A beautiful blonde woman smiled back at her from the screen. The same woman who'd been in the picture in Carson's bedroom. Emma Christensen, according to the caption. Engaged to Carson Crest. Deceased.

And then she saw the video. A charity event, a little over four years ago. She remembered it vaguely. She'd been filming for her social media, capturing the atmosphere, the people. In the video, Emma was having what appeared to be a breakdown, while Kinsley, oblivious, filmed in the background.

The next document was a news article about Emma's suicide.

The pieces clicked into place as tears fell down her cheeks. Carson never truly wanted to help her. Not really. He'd wanted her to fall from grace.

Kinsley pushed back from the desk, her body trembling. The man she'd been falling for had been methodically destroying her life for years. Everything—the contract, the fake relationship, the sex—it had all been part of his plan.

She'd been such a fool.

Hot tears streamed down her face, but she wiped them away furiously. No. She was done crying. Done being manipulated. Done being the victim.

She glanced around the office, spotting her purse on the couch. Her phone was still in there. She grabbed it, shoving it into her pocket without checking it. She needed to get out. Now.

But first, she took out a piece of paper from Carson's desk and scribbled a note.

I saw everything. How could you do this to me? You're sick, and I hope you burn for this. I hope it was worth it. Fuck you, Carson.

She left it on his keyboard where he couldn't miss it, right beneath the picture of Emma still left open on the screen.

Kinsley peeked out of the office door. The hallway was clear. She slipped out, heart pounding, and made her way toward the elevator. A group of employees rounded the corner, and she ducked into a stairwell.

Twenty-seven flights of stairs later, she emerged in the lobby, breathless but determined. She kept her head down, sunglasses on, as she navigated through the space. No one stopped her. No one seemed to notice her slip out a side door.

Outside, the bright afternoon sun momentarily blinded her. The city bustled, oblivious to her world collapsing, once again thanks to Carson Fucking Crest. She started walking, no destination in mind, just away. Away from Carson. Away from the lies. Away from the person she'd become.

Her phone buzzed in her pocket. She ignored it. It buzzed again, insistently. Finally, she pulled it out.

Fifteen missed calls from Carson. Ten text messages.

Kinsley, where are you?

Please answer your phone.

It's not safe for you to be alone right now.

There's more going on than you know.

Please, let me explain.

She turned off her phone and dropped it in a trash can as she passed. She wouldn't give him the satisfaction of tracking her.

As she walked, the initial shock crystallized into something harder, sharper. Anger. No, rage. Pure, incandescent rage. At Carson, yes, but also at herself. For being so desperate for approval that she'd walked right into his trap. For being so easily manipulated. For believing she needed someone else to save her.

No more. She was no longer that girl.

She'd rebuild, on her own terms this time. No more pandering, no more perfect facade. She'd tell her truth, the real truth, not the carefully curated version she'd been selling for years.

If she went down, it would be as herself. Not as Carson's puppet.

She turned down an alley, a shortcut to the main avenue where she could lose herself in the crowd. Her mind raced with plans. She needed cash, a place to stay that couldn't be traced back to her, a way to tell her story before Carson could spin it.

Because he would. Clearly that had been the plan the entire time. Fuck her and then fuck her life up.

The sound of tires on wet pavement behind her made her turn. A black SUV had pulled into the alley, blocking the way she'd come. Before she could run, three men in balaclavas jumped out.

"Hello Ms. Ellis," one of them said as he reached for her.

Kinsley opened her mouth to scream, but a gloved hand clamped over it. Strong arms lifted her off her feet as she kicked and thrashed.

"Got her," another voice said. "Let's go before someone sees."

They bundled her into the SUV, the door slamming shut behind them. As the vehicle accelerated, Kinsley's last thought before a cloth covered her face was bitter irony. After everything Carson had done to her, someone else would be the one to finish her off.

The world went black.

CHAPTER ELEVEN

CARSON

CARSON BROKE EVERY SINGLE OBJECT IN HIS OFFICE IN less than two minutes. He'd stared at the laptop screen, Kinsley's note burning into his retinas.

I saw everything. How could you do this to me? You're sick, and I hope you burn for this. I hope it was worth it. Fuck you, Carson.

His hands shook as he closed the laptop. The tremors spread up his arms, through his chest, and into his throat where they transformed into a guttural roar that tore through the office. In one violent motion, he hurled the laptop against the wall, watching it shatter into a spray of plastic and metal.

"Carson!" Benedict rushed in, eyes wide. "What the hell—"

Carson upended his desk, sending everything crashing to the floor. His carefully organized files, his precisely arranged pens, the sleek desktop monitor—all of it scattered across the carpet. He grabbed his chair and slammed it against the bookshelf, causing framed accolades and business awards to rain down in a cascade of broken glass.

"She knows." The words felt like razors in his throat. "She knows everything."

Benedict stood frozen in the doorway, eyes wide as Carson's fist crashed through a framed photo on the wall. Glass rained down, blood smearing across the jagged edges of the broken frame.

"Carson, stop. Just—" Benedict stepped over a toppled lamp. "What the hell happened? What do you mean she knows?"

Carson couldn't speak. His throat felt raw from screaming. Every object, every meticulously arranged piece of his controlled environment lay in ruins around him. Just like his plans.

"Kinsley found out."

Penn appeared in the doorway behind Benedict, laptop clutched to his chest, eyes darting between the two men and the chaos surrounding them. "What in the shit happened in here?"

Carson sank to his knees among the wreckage, a shard of glass cutting into his palm as he braced himself against the floor. The pain barely registered. "I did this. All of it."

Benedict crouched beside him, careful to avoid the debris. "Did what, exactly? Talk to me."

Carson looked up, meeting his friend's concerned gaze. The weight of four and a half years of deception pressed down on him until his lungs felt as though they'd shriveled up. "I'm the reason the world canceled Kinsley Ellis. I'm the one who orchestrated her fall from grace. All of it—the sponsors dropping her, the leaked conversations, the public turning against her. It was me."

Penn's mouth fell open. "What are you talking about?"

"For years," Carson continued, his voice hollow. "Since Emma died. Kinsley was there at that gala. She filmed the breakdown that went viral. She posted it where everyone could see. Where everyone could bully Emma into taking her own life. I blamed Kinsley for Emma." He laughed bitterly. "And now Kinsley's gone. She found out everything, and she ran. It's my fucking fault."

Benedict's expression hardened. "You're telling me this whole time, it was all just revenge? The contract, the fake relationship?"

"It started that way." Carson pushed himself to his feet, ignoring the blood dripping from his hand. "But then I got to know her. And I —" He couldn't finish the sentence. What could he say? That he'd fallen for the woman he'd tried to destroy?

Penn was frantically typing on his laptop. "I'm pulling up the security feeds. If she left the building, we'll find her."

Benedict stared at Carson, disappointment etched across his features. "Does Paisley know about this? She's friends with Kinsley."

"No one knew." Carson paced through the debris, kicking items in his way. "Not you, not Paisley, no one. I kept it separate from the company. Personal."

"Personal?" Benedict's voice rose. "You used our resources, our reputation—"

"I know what I did!" Carson shouted, slamming his fist against the wall. "And now she's gone, and she's out there alone while someone is actively threatening her. God, I messed up."

"Yeah, I'd say." Benedict stood in the middle of the room with his arms crossed. "What the hell, Cars? Why didn't you tell me?"

"What, like you'd help?" Carson scoffed, shaking his head. "I ruined Kinsley's life and then I went and fell in love with her like a fucking idiot, thinking none of what I'd done would matter. Not if she never found out. But guess what?"

"She found out." Benedict spoke in a flat tone, running a hand through his sandy blonde hair with a sigh. "Fuck, Carson. This is bad."

"No shit, Sherlock. I—"

"Found her!" Penn's voice cut through their argument. "I've got her on the street cameras."

Both men rushed to Penn's side, crowding around his laptop screen. The grainy footage showed Kinsley exiting the building, her face streaked with tears as she hurried down the sidewalk.

"She's headed east," Penn narrated, fingers flying across the keyboard as he switched between camera feeds. "There she is turning down—wait, she's going into that alley."

They watched as Kinsley disappeared into the narrow passage between buildings. Penn switched to another camera angle, but the alley remained empty.

"Where is she?" Carson demanded. "Switch to the other end."

Penn pulled up another feed. "There's no exit camera for that alley, but I can see the street." He pointed to the screen. "Black SUV, tinted windows. It just pulled out of the alley."

Carson felt his blood turn to ice. "And Kinsley?"

"She hasn't come out." Penn's voice was grim. "The SUV entered and left."

"Fuck!" Carson slammed his hand on the desk. "Run the plates, now!"

Benedict already had his phone out. "Jenna, we have a situation. Kinsley Ellis disappeared out of the office and was scene going down an alley, but wasn't seen coming out of it. There was a vehicle. It may be an abduction. Yes, back side. Black SUV, Penn's sending you the details. Get a team ready." He paused, listening. "Yes, immediately."

Penn continued typing. "The plates are fake. I'm running facial recognition on the driver, but the angle is bad."

Carson's phone buzzed in his pocket. He pulled it out, seeing an unknown number on the screen. Below it was a text message that had arrived earlier—the one that had pulled him away from Kinsley, giving her the opportunity to discover his secrets.

He opened the text and his stomach dropped. It contained a photo taken through his office window. Kinsley on her knees before him, her lips wrapped around his cock. The message below read:

> I see everything. Your pretty little influencer looks good like this. Wonder what she'd look like broken?

His phone rang again, the same unknown number. Carson answered, forcing his voice to remain steady. "This is Crest."

"You should have kept a closer eye on your toy." The voice was digitally altered to sound deeper. "She ran right into our arms."

Carson's jaw clenched. "Who is this?"

"Not a friend, Crest." The voice laughed. "But I'll give you a chance to get her back."

Benedict and Penn were watching him even as Benedict called Tanner and James.

Carson kept his expression neutral. "I'm listening."

"Warehouse 17, Brooklyn Navy Yard. Midnight. Come alone or she dies. No police, no security team, no partners. Just you."

"How do I know she's alive?" Carson demanded in a quieter voice, turning his back on Benedict and Penn.

There was a pause, then Kinsley's voice came through the speaker. "Get off me you piece of shit. I swear I'm going to—"

Her voice cut off abruptly, replaced by the distorted one. "Midnight. Alone. Don't be late."

The call ended. Carson lowered the phone slowly, his mind racing.

"Who was that?" Benedict asked.

"Wrong number." Carson slipped the phone back into his pocket. "Penn, keep working on identifying that vehicle. I need to clean up."

He walked to the private bathroom attached to his office, closing the door behind him. His reflection in the mirror looked like a stranger. A pale, wild-eyed, blood smeared stranger. He ran his injured hand under cold water, watching the pink swirl down the drain.

Four hours until midnight. Four hours to figure out how to get Kinsley back without getting them both killed.

Carson cleaned and bandaged his wounds, his mind working through scenarios. He couldn't tell Benedict or Penn—they'd insist on sending a team, and that would get Kinsley killed. He couldn't risk Jenna's security personnel either. Maybe Tanner could be back up. Or James. They'd both been military. But no. This was his mess, his responsibility.

His phone buzzed again. Another text from the unknown number.

> Tick tock. Come alone or we send these photos to every news outlet in the country. And then we send pieces of her.

Attached was another photo. Kinsley bound to a chair, a bruise forming on her cheek, terror in her eyes.

Carson's hand tightened around the phone until his knuckles turned white. He'd done this. His obsession with revenge had put her in danger. If anything happened to her...

He splashed cold water on his face, steadying himself. He needed to be calm, focused. Kinsley needed him to think clearly whether she hated him or not.

She was his to protect.

He'd get her back.

He had to.

When he emerged from the bathroom, Benedict and Penn huddled around the laptop, deep in conversation.

"Any progress?" Carson asked, his voice deliberately casual.

Penn shook his head. "The SUV disappeared into a blind spot in Red Hook. We're still searching."

"I need to get some air," Carson announced. "Clear my head."

Benedict looked up, concern evident in his expression. "Carson, Jenna isn't here with her team to protect you, and this isn't the time to—"

"I can't think in here," Carson gestured to the destroyed office. "I need space. Keep working. Call me if you find anything. I'll be careful."

Before either man could protest further, Carson strode out, grabbing his coat from the hook by the door. In the elevator, he checked his watch. Three hours and forty minutes until midnight.

He took his personal car from the garage, a sleek black Audi that he rarely drove in the city. As he navigated through Manhattan traffic toward the Brooklyn Bridge, his mind kept returning to Kinsley's face. Not the terrified expression from the kidnapper's photo, but the look of betrayal and hurt when she must have discovered his plans on his laptop.

He'd been so consumed with making her pay that he hadn't seen what was happening until it was too late. He'd fallen for her. The woman he'd set out to destroy had somehow become essential to him.

And now she was in danger because of him.

Carson gripped the steering wheel tighter. He had no illusions about what awaited him at the warehouse. This wasn't just about Kinsley. Someone wanted him there, alone and vulnerable. Someone who'd been watching them closely enough to photograph them through his office windows. Someone who knew exactly how to hurt him. She was a means to an end, and that meant that to these people, she was expendable.

Not to him.

As he crossed the Brooklyn Bridge, the Manhattan skyline glittering behind him, Carson made a decision. He would get Kinsley out alive, whatever it took.

He pulled over in a quiet spot in Brooklyn Heights and made a call to his lawyer, quickly updating his will. He accessed a hidden app on his phone, activating a GPS tracker embedded in his watch. Benedict might not know where he was going, but if things went wrong, at least they'd find his body.

His final call was to a secure storage facility in Queens. Twenty minutes later, he parked outside a nondescript building, punching in a code at a keypad. Inside, he opened a small safe and removed a matte black Glock 19 and a silencer, checking that it was loaded before tucking it into a shoulder holster under his jacket.

Back in the car, Carson checked his watch again. Two hours until midnight. Enough time to scout the location without being detected.

As he drove toward the Brooklyn Navy Yard, his phone rang. Benedict's name flashed on the screen. Carson hesitated, then answered.

"Where the hell are you?" Benedict demanded without preamble.

"Taking care of something," Carson replied.

"Bullshit. Penn traced your car heading to Brooklyn. That call wasn't a wrong number, was it? They contacted you about Kinsley."

Carson remained silent.

"Carson, don't be stupid," Benedict continued. "We can help. Jenna's team is ready. Just tell us where you're going."

"I can't," Carson finally said. "They'll kill her if I don't come alone."

"And they'll kill you both if you do!" Benedict's voice rose in frustration. "This isn't a negotiation situation, Carson. These people are clearly professionals."

"I know," Carson said quietly. "That's why I have to do this my way. I got her into this mess. I'll get her out."

"Carson—"

"Take care of Paisley for me if this goes sideways." Carson's voice was steady. "And if something happens to me, tell Kinsley... tell her I'm sorry. For everything."

He ended the call and turned off his phone, tossing it onto the passenger seat. The Brooklyn Navy Yard loomed ahead, its abandoned warehouses dark against the night sky.

Time to get his woman back.

CHAPTER TWELVE

CARSON

Carson parked the Audi three blocks from Warehouse 17, killing the headlights before he reached the perimeter of the Navy Yard. The industrial complex was a ghost town at night, which of course made it perfect for the kind of meeting that ended with bodies.

He checked his watch: 11:27 PM.

The weight of the Glock pressed against his ribs as he moved through the shadows, staying low and using the abandoned equipment and shipping containers as cover. His senses heightened in the low light. He wasn't as trained as some of his friends, but he wasn't an idiot either. Carson cataloged his surroundings, the distant hum of the BQE, the lap of water against the docks, the occasional screech of gulls.

Warehouse 17 was a massive concrete structure with broken windows. Someone had parked a black SUV by the side entrance, its windows tinted to opacity.

Carson circled the building, noting the entrances and exits. Two men stood smoking outside a loading bay, their postures casual but their eyes alert. Each had a handgun holstered at his hip.

He attached the silencer to his Glock. The shooting range was a poor substitute for actual combat experience, but Carson had always been a quick study. Tanner had taught him more than just how to hit a target, but he still felt anxious as he lifted the gun.

The first guard went down with a muffled thud, the bullet catching him in the chest. The second had just enough time to reach for his weapon before Carson's second shot found its mark.

Tanner would've been proud.

Or horrified.

But mostly proud.

Carson dragged both bodies behind a stack of pallets, his heart hammering against his ribs. The metallic smell of blood filled his nostrils, making his stomach lurch. He'd never killed before. It felt nothing like the clean paper targets at the range.

He took the first guard's radio, clipping it to his belt, and entered the warehouse through the loading bay.

Inside, the cavernous space was mostly dark, save for a pool of harsh light in the center where portable construction lamps had been set up. Carson crouched behind a stack of rusted metal barrels.

He froze.

Kinsley hung suspended from a chain attached to an overhead beam, her toes barely touching the concrete floor. Her wrists were bound above her head, angry red marks visible where the rope had cut into her skin. Her face was streaked with tears and dirt. Fire burned in her eyes, though, and her expression remained one of defiance rather than defeat.

Five men circled her like wolves around wounded prey. One held what looked like a cattle prod, its end crackling with blue electricity.

"Let's try again, sweetheart," the man said, pressing the prod against Kinsley's side.

Her scream, muffled by the gag in her mouth, tore through Carson. He gripped the Glock tighter, forcing himself to remain still, to think. Five against one. He needed a plan, not blind rage.

"Boss says pretty boy should be here by midnight," another man said, checking his watch. "Shouldn't we save some of the fun for when he arrives?"

"Relax. We've got plenty of time to play with both of them." The first man who was taller than the others, with a shaved head and a jagged scar running from his ear to his chin circled Kinsley. "Besides, I want her nice and cooperative when her little boyfriend shows up."

"You sure he's coming?" A third heavyset man with a thick beard seemed more skeptical. "What if he doesn't give a shit about her?"

Scar Face laughed. "Trust me, he'll come. You don't make the kind of enemies our employer has without being predictable in some ways. Carson Crest thinks he's untouchable, but he's got one weakness now." He ran a finger down Kinsley's cheek. "And we've got her."

Kinsley jerked her head away from his touch.

"The man loves her," Scar Face continued. "And love makes you stupid. He'll walk right through our door, trying to play hero."

Carson's mind raced. They were right. He had absolutely walked into their trap. But they didn't know he was already here, watching. That gave him an advantage, however slight.

Scar Face yanked the gag from Kinsley's mouth. "Maybe you'd like to tell us what he's like in bed? Pass the time while we wait?"

Kinsley spat directly in his face. "You're fucking idiots if you think Carson is coming for me."

The man wiped the spittle from his cheek, his expression darkening. "Is that so?"

"He's the one who destroyed my life," Kinsley said, her voice raw. God, how much had she screamed to make it sound like that? "He never loved me. We fucked. That was it. You're wasting your time and mine."

Hearing her say the truth of what he'd done to her out loud made him hate himself with a ferocity that rivaled his earlier hatred of her.

Scar Face backhanded her across the face, hard enough to split her lip. "Lying bitch. We've been watching you two for weeks. The way he looks at you, that's not just fucking."

Kinsley laughed a hollow laugh, shaking her head. "You don't know him. Carson Crest doesn't care about anyone but himself. Trust me, I learned that the hard way."

Another man stepped forward, running his hands over Kinsley's body in a way that made Carson's finger twitch on the trigger. "Maybe we should show her what real men are like, eh, Lester? Teach her boyfriend a lesson when he shows up."

"Keep your dick in your pants," Scar Face—Lester—snapped. "We're professionals. Besides..." He gripped Kinsley's chin, forcing her to look at him. "I think our girl here is playing tough. Look at those eyes. She's already broken inside. Aren't you, sweetheart?"

Kinsley stared back at him, unflinching. "Go to hell."

Carson surveyed the warehouse again. The five men were arranged in a rough circle around Kinsley. Lester and the one who'd touched Kinsley—Handsy, Carson decided—stood closest to her. Two others were slightly further back, while the fifth man who was shorter than the others hovered near what looked like a table of equipment.

Carson formulated a plan. He moved silently through the shadows, positioning himself behind a forklift about twenty feet from the nervous man. One clean shot. That's all he needed.

Carson steadied his breathing, aimed, and fired.

The man dropped without a sound, a neat hole in the center of his forehead.

Before the others could react, Carson had already shifted his aim to another one, who was turning toward his fallen comrade with confusion written across his face. The second shot caught him in the throat.

Chaos erupted. Lester and Handsy drew their weapons, shouting in what sounded like Russian. The man with the beard dove behind a stack of crates, firing blindly in Carson's direction.

Carson ducked as bullets splintered the forklift beside him. His heart raced, and he forced himself to take a deep breath. Every gunshot, though, had him flinching. He rolled to a new position, coming up with his gun trained on Lester, who was using Kinsley as a human shield.

"Come out, Crest!" Lester shouted. "Or we start cutting pieces off your girlfriend!"

Carson's mind raced. He needed a distraction. His gaze fell on a pile of oil drums about ten feet to his left. One well-placed shot...

He fired, and the drum erupted in flames as the bullet ignited whatever was inside. In the momentary confusion, Carson sprinted toward a new position, closer to Kinsley.

From his new vantage point, he could see her face clearly for the first time. Her eyes widened in genuine shock when she spotted him.

Beard emerged from behind the crates, firing without aiming. Carson dropped him with two shots to the chest.

Three down, two to go.

But he'd lost track of Handsy in the chaos. Carson scanned the warehouse frantically, only to feel the cold press of metal against the back of his head.

"Drop the gun, hero," Handsy's voice was cold.

Carson hesitated, calculating his odds. They weren't good.

"I said drop it!" The gun pressed harder. "Or Lester puts a bullet in her pretty face."

Carson let his gun clatter to the floor. Handsy kicked it away, then slammed the butt of his own gun into the back of Carson's head.

Pain exploded behind his eyes as he stumbled forward. Another blow caught him in the kidney, sending him to his knees.

"Bring him here," Lester ordered.

Handsy grabbed Carson by the collar, dragging him to the center of the light where Kinsley hung. Up close, her injuries were worse than he'd thought. Bruises formed on her arms and face, burn marks from the cattle prod visible through her torn shirt.

"So the boyfriend did show up after all," Lester circled him, gloating. "Just like our employer said you would."

Carson spat blood onto the concrete. "Who hired you?"

"Someone you pissed off very badly." Lester nodded to Handsy, who delivered a vicious kick to Carson's ribs. "Someone who wants you to suffer before you die."

Another kick. Something cracked inside his chest, likely a broken rib. The pain was blinding.

"Stop it!" Kinsley shouted, straining against her bonds. "Leave him alone!"

Lester laughed. "Look at that. She does care after all." He grabbed a handful of Carson's hair, yanking his head back. "You two deserve each other. Liars, both of you."

Carson locked eyes with Kinsley. Despite everything, despite knowing what he'd done to her, she was trying to protect him.

He'd never deserved her. Not for a single moment.

"Now, let's have some real fun," Lester said, pulling a knife from his boot. The blade gleamed in the harsh light. "Our employer didn't specify what condition your body needed to be in, just that you needed to die. Slowly."

Carson watched the knife approach his face, his mind racing. One chance. That's all he had.

He lunged suddenly, headbutting Lester in the stomach. The man stumbled back, winded. Carson rolled, grabbing for the knife that had clattered to the floor.

His fingers closed around the handle just as Handsy tackled him. They grappled on the concrete. Carson managed to flip their positions, driving the knife into Handsy's chest.

The man's eyes widened in surprise, then glazed over as death claimed him.

Carson staggered to his feet, knife in hand, only to freeze as Lester pressed his gun to Kinsley's temple.

"Drop it, Crest," Lester's voice remained calm. "Or I paint the walls with her brains."

Carson's gaze met Kinsley's. Her eyes were wide. She gave an almost imperceptible shake of her head, telling him not to surrender.

But he couldn't risk her life. Not for anything.

The knife clattered to the floor.

"On your knees," Lester ordered.

Carson complied, his body screaming in protest as he knelt before Kinsley. Lester moved to stand behind him, the gun now pressed to the back of Carson's head.

"Our employer will be pleased," Viktor said. "The great Carson Crest, brought low by a woman. It's almost poetic."

"Who hired you?" Carson asked again, playing for time.

"Someone who knows your secrets. Someone who's been watching you for a very long time." Lester chuckled. "Any last words?"

Carson looked up at Kinsley, taking in every detail of her face as if to memorize it for whatever came after death. Her defiant hazel eyes. The curve of her cheek. The strength in her jaw.

"I'm sorry," he said softly. "For everything I did to you. I set out to destroy you because I thought you were responsible for Emma's death. I was wrong. So wrong." His voice broke. "And somewhere along the way, I fell in love with you. The real you. Not the persona I thought I hated."

Tears spilled down Kinsley's cheeks. "Carson—"

"I love you, Kinsley Ellis," Carson said, his voice steady despite the gun at his head. "With everything I am. And I'm sorry I won't get the chance to prove it to you."

The shot rang out.

CHAPTER THIRTEEN

KINSLEY

KINSLEY LOST TRACK OF HOW MUCH SHE'D SCREAMED. BUT this one was the loudest. No damn cattle prod could make her throat raw like when she heard the gun go off.

The gunshot exploded in Kinsley's ears, her scream tearing through her. Kinsley's eyes slammed shut. A reflex, not a choice. It was as if they refused to witness Carson's death.

One second. Two seconds.

No thud. No sound of Carson's body hitting the warehouse floor.

Kinsley forced her eyes open, confusion replacing terror as she saw Carson still standing, eyes wide with the same shock she felt. Then Lester crumpled sideways, his gun clattering uselessly to the concrete.

Behind where he'd stood was a tall woman with auburn hair pulled back in a tight braid. She lowered her weapon. Recognition flickered through Kinsley's exhausted brain. The security professional from Crest Strategies. The one who'd escorted them through the reporters. Kinsley couldn't remember her name.

"Clear the perimeter," the woman barked into her earpiece. "Hostiles down inside, targets secured."

Kinsley's body went limp against the chains holding her upright, relief flooding through her like a drug. Her muscles, tensed for hours against pain and fear, surrendered all at once.

Carson lunged toward her, his face littered with bruises and blood. His right eye was swelling shut, lip split, but he moved with surprising speed for someone who'd just been beaten half to death. He reached up, fumbling with the padlock securing her chains.

"Keys," he rasped. He scrambled back to the body, patting Lester's pockets with shaking hands. Finding them, he unlocked her restraints.

The moment the chains released, Kinsley's legs buckled. She dropped like a stone, but Carson caught her before she hit the ground, his arms encircling her. He lowered them both to the floor, cradling her against his chest.

"I've got you," he whispered against her hair. "I've got you."

His lips found hers, tasting of blood and salt. Kinsley froze, her body going rigid in his arms. The kiss wasn't painful, at least not physically. But it lanced through her heart nonetheless.

How could he still feel like home when he'd been the one to burn her house down?

"Let go of me." The words came out flat, emotionless. "Please."

Carson stiffened, then slowly pulled back. The unguarded look of hurt in his eyes didn't seem right. It wasn't one of the calculated expressions she'd grown accustomed to. He didn't argue, didn't try to convince her. He simply loosened his grip and helped her sit upright on the cold concrete floor.

"Right," he said, voice barely audible.

The warehouse filled with tactical personnel in black. The auburn-haired woman approached, holstering her weapon.

"Mr. Crest, Ms. Ellis," she said, kneeling beside them. "We need to get you both medical attention."

"I'm fine, Jenna," Carson said automatically.

Jenna ignored him. "Can you walk, Ms. Ellis?"

Kinsley tried to stand, but her legs trembled violently. The cattle prod had done its work well, leaving her muscles spasming and unreliable.

"I can carry—" Carson began.

"No," Kinsley cut him off. The thought of being in his arms again made her chest ache with a confusion she couldn't process in that moment. "Just... help me up."

Jenna slipped an arm around Kinsley's waist, supporting her weight. "We have a medical team outside. Let's get you there."

As they made their slow way out of the warehouse, Kinsley couldn't help glancing back at Carson. He stood watching them, blood dripping from his temple, looking utterly lost. For a heartbeat, she almost called out to him, almost asked him to come with her.

Instead, she turned away and focused on putting one foot in front of the other.

Outside, the cold night air hit her face. The waterfront was alive with flashing lights. Police cars, ambulances, black SUVs with tinted windows. Jenna guided her toward one of the medical vans.

"We're taking you back to the office building," Jenna explained. "We have a private physician who will treat you there. It's more secure."

Kinsley nodded numbly, too exhausted to argue. As paramedics helped her into the van, she caught sight of Carson emerging from the warehouse, flanked by two of Jenna's team. He looked smaller somehow, diminished. When their eyes met across the distance, she quickly looked away.

The ride back to Crest Strategies passed in a blur. Kinsley stared out the window, watching Manhattan's lights smear together through the glass. Her body ached everywhere. Her shoulders screamed from being suspended, her skin littered with angry red welts from the cattle prod, her wrists rubbed raw from the restraints.

But those pains were nothing compared to the hollow ache in her chest.

Carson had destroyed her. And it seemed the last thing he'd ripped away from her was her ability to love. He'd monitored her, manipulated her, orchestrated her downfall, all for revenge over a woman Kinsley barely remembered filming.

And then he'd fallen in love with her.

Or claimed to. How could she believe anything he said now?

Yet the way he'd looked on his knees, apologizing and telling her he loved her... That hadn't been calculation. The way he'd whispered "I love you" with a gun to his head hadn't sounded like a lie.

Jenna helped Kinsley into a private elevator that bypassed the main floors, taking them directly to what appeared to be a secure medical suite.

A gray-haired woman with kind eyes introduced herself as Dr. Nikelson and guided Kinsley to an examination table. The doctor worked efficiently, cleaning wounds, applying ointments to burns, checking for signs of concussion.

"You're dehydrated," she said, inserting an IV into Kinsley's arm. "And these electrical burns need treatment, but you'll heal. Physically, at least." She squeezed Kinsley's hand gently. "The rest takes time."

After the examination, Jenna showed her to a small but comfortable room adjacent to the medical suite. "You can rest here. There's a bathroom through that door with everything you might need. I'll be right outside if you need anything."

"Thank you," Kinsley said, her voice still raw.

Jenna nodded and left, closing the door quietly behind her.

Alone at last, Kinsley sank onto the edge of the bed. She should have been crying. That would have made sense. But her eyes remained dry, as if her body had run out of ways to express pain.

She didn't know how long she sat there, staring at nothing, when a soft knock came at the door.

"Kinsley?" A familiar voice, but not Carson's. "It's Paisley. Can I come in?"

Kinsley hesitated, then called out, "Yes."

The door opened, and Paisley stepped in, her brown eyes wide. She was chewing on her thumbnail.

"Thank goodness your alive," Paisley breathed, rushing forward. "Are you okay? I mean, obviously you're not okay, but—" She stopped herself, hovering uncertainly. "Can I hug you? Or would that hurt too much?"

Despite everything, Kinsley felt her lips curve into a small smile. "A gentle hug would be nice."

Paisley's arms came around her carefully, and Kinsley leaned into the embrace, suddenly grateful for human contact that wasn't complicated.

"I was so scared," Paisley whispered, pulling back to look at her. "When Benedict called and told me what happened..." She shook her head. "I'm just glad you're safe."

Kinsley nodded, not trusting herself to speak.

Paisley perched beside her on the bed. "I don't know exactly what's going on between you and my brother," she said slowly. "But I know enough to guess it's complicated."

"That's one word for it," Kinsley said, her voice flat.

Paisley twisted her hands in her lap. "I want to tell you something about Emma."

The name sent a chill through Kinsley. Emma. The reason for everything.

"Emma was..." Paisley paused, searching for words. "She was beautiful. Inside and out. She had this laugh that made everyone around her smile. But she struggled. God, did she struggle."

Paisley's eyes grew distant. "She had anxiety and depression her whole life. I remember the first time I met her, she had to step out of the restaurant three times to breathe through panic attacks. Carson was so patient with her. He never made her feel bad about it."

Kinsley listened, a knot forming in her throat.

"Things got worse over the years, not better," Paisley continued. "She'd have good months, then crash. The doctors kept changing her medications, but nothing seemed to help long-term. The week before she died, she'd been hospitalized after a particularly bad episode."

Paisley's voice cracked. "When that video went viral, the one where she was having a breakdown in the background, it was just the final straw. She couldn't bear being exposed that way, having strangers comment on her most vulnerable moment."

"I didn't know she was in my video," Kinsley whispered. "I swear I didn't even notice her."

"I didn't realize it was your video until later. And I believe you," Paisley said softly. "But Carson... losing Emma broke something in him. He'd spent years trying to protect her, trying to fix things, and then suddenly she was gone. He needed somewhere to put all that pain."

Kinsley wrapped her arms around herself. "So he put it on me."

"I'm not excusing what he did," Paisley said quickly. "Whatever he did. And honestly, I don't know the details. I'm not here to justify it. But I haven't seen my brother truly happy in four years. Not until recently." She met Kinsley's eyes. "Not until you."

Kinsley looked away.

"Carson loves hard," Paisley said. "He can't do anything halfway. It's just not in his DNA. When he commits to something, he's all in. It's what makes him brilliant at his job, and sometimes terrible at being human."

A reluctant laugh escaped Kinsley's lips.

"I'm not asking you to forgive him today," Paisley continued. "Maybe not tomorrow or next week either. Just... someday. Consider it. Because the man who went into that warehouse alone to save you? That's the real Carson. The one who's been hiding under all that anger and pain."

Kinsley didn't respond, but she didn't need to. Paisley seemed to understand the silence.

"And for what it's worth," Paisley added, "I hope we can still be friends. I've missed you."

"I'd like that," Kinsley said, surprised to find she meant it. "But where have you been? I tried texting you a few times before... everything."

Paisley's expression turned apologetic. "I know, and I'm sorry. I've been looking into something big. It's taken all my time." She chewed her thumbnail again. "I can't talk about it yet, but hopefully soon."

She stood, giving Kinsley's hand a gentle squeeze. "Get some rest. And remember what I said. Not about forgiving him. That's your choice. But about us being friends."

"I will," Kinsley promised.

After Paisley left, Kinsley lay back on the bed, staring at the ceiling.

Her body ached for sleep, but her mind raced with everything Paisley had told her.

Emma had been ill. Truly, deeply ill. And while that didn't excuse what Carson had done, it colored everything with shades of grief Kinsley hadn't considered before. He hadn't just lost someone he loved. He'd lost someone he'd been trying desperately to save.

And then he'd fallen in love with the very person he blamed.

Kinsley closed her eyes, too exhausted to untangle the mess of emotions swirling inside her. She didn't know if she could forgive Carson. She didn't know if what they'd shared had been real or just another manipulation that had backfired.

She only knew that right now, she needed space to breathe. Space to heal. Space to decide who she wanted to be after all of this.

Sleep finally claimed her, but not before one last thought drifted through her mind:

The man who'd whispered "I love you" with a gun to his head hadn't been lying.

CHAPTER FOURTEEN

CARSON

A WEEK WENT BY WITHOUT A WORD FROM KINSLEY. AND then another. Carson had asked Benedict to work with Jenna to find a safe place for her to heal. He didn't know where it was. Hadn't bothered trying to find it.

Carson stared into the amber depths of his glass, the brandy catching firelight like liquid gold. He'd been sitting there for—hell, he didn't even know anymore. Days had begun blurring into nights, marked only by the steady emptying of bottles and the hollow echo of his thoughts.

His penthouse felt cavernous around him. Too quiet. Too empty. The silence pressed against his eardrums until he could hear his own heartbeat. It was a dull thud that reminded him he was still alive when he'd rather not be.

Three weeks since Kinsley had disappeared from his life. Three weeks of nothing but the knowledge that he'd destroyed the one good thing that had accidentally grown in the wasteland of his revenge.

Carson dug his hand into the cereal box beside him, shoving a handful of dry flakes into his mouth without tasting them. The brandy burned his throat on the way down.

His phone lay face-down on the coffee table. He'd stopped

checking it days ago. What was the point? Benedict sent updates. Kinsley was safe, Kinsley was healing, Kinsley wanted nothing to do with him.

It was Emma all over again. Only worse, because this time, there was no one to blame but himself.

He'd built his entire existence around avenging Emma, around making Kinsley pay for a sin she'd never actually committed. And in doing so, he'd become something far worse than she'd ever been.

The fireplace crackled, sending shadows dancing across the walls. Carson ran a hand through his unwashed hair, feeling the stubble that had grown into something more substantial on his jaw. When had he last showered? Eaten something that wasn't cereal straight from the box?

The intercom buzzed.

Carson ignored it.

It buzzed again, more insistent this time.

"Fuck off," he muttered, taking another swig of brandy.

The buzzing continued.

With a growl, Carson pushed himself off the couch, swaying slightly as he crossed to the intercom panel. His finger jabbed the button with more force than necessary.

"What?" he snapped.

A beat of silence. "It's me."

Kinsley.

Carson's breath caught in his throat. His heart hammered against his ribs, suddenly too big for his chest.

"Carson?" Her voice again, uncertain this time.

He realized he hadn't responded, had just been standing there, frozen in disbelief.

"I'm sending the elevator," he managed, pressing the button with a shaking finger.

Carson backed away from the panel, suddenly acutely aware of his disheveled state. Shirtless, wearing only boxers, unshaven, reeking of alcohol. He glanced around frantically, as if a clean shirt might materialize out of thin air.

Too late. The elevator was already on its way up.

He raked his fingers through his hair. What was she doing here? Had she come to tell him off properly? To demand more answers? To make sure he was suffering?

The thought struck him that he didn't care. Whatever her reason, he'd take it. Just to see her face again.

The elevator chimed.

The doors slid open.

Kinsley stood there, hesitant, one hand still on the elevator door as if ready to retreat. She looked thinner, shadows beneath her eyes that hadn't been there before. But god, she was beautiful. So beautiful it hurt to look at her.

"Kinsley," he breathed.

She stepped into his penthouse, letting the elevator doors close behind her. Kinsley took in his appearance, his obvious disarray, the bottle on the coffee table.

"You look like shit," she said finally.

"Yeah."

They stood in awkward silence for far too long.

"Why are you here?" Carson asked finally.

Kinsley's hands twisted together. "I don't know." She shook her head. "No, that's a lie. I do know. I just... I need answers. Real ones."

Carson nodded, gesturing toward the couch. "Do you want to sit?"

She hesitated, then moved to perch on the edge of the couch, as far from his abandoned spot as possible. Carson remained standing, suddenly unable to imagine sitting beside her as if they were having a normal conversation.

"I'm listening," he said.

Kinsley looked up at him, and the pain in her eyes nearly brought him to his knees.

"Why me?" she asked simply. "All these years. All this... hatred. Why?"

Carson's throat tightened. "I thought—" He stopped, shook his head. "No. No more lies, no more excuses. I blamed you for Emma's death because it was easier than blaming myself."

He turned away, unable to meet her gaze. "I couldn't save Emma. I couldn't fix her depression, her anxiety. I tried everything, and nothing worked. And then she saw that video, with her breakdown in the background, and she..." His voice cracked. "A few days later, she was gone."

Carson faced Kinsley again, forcing himself to look her in the eye. "I needed someone to blame. Someone to punish. And you were there. The person who filmed it, who posted it. It was easier to hate you than to face the truth."

"Which was what?" Kinsley's voice was barely above a whisper.

"That I failed her." How could words hurt so bad? "That I wasn't enough. That maybe nothing would have been enough. And I couldn't live with that, so I turned it all on you."

Kinsley stood abruptly, anger flashing in her eyes. "You ruined my life because you couldn't handle your own guilt?"

"Yes." The simple admission hung in the air.

"Do you have any idea what you've done to me?" Her voice rose. "You stalked me for years. You manipulated me, isolated me from everyone I cared about. You made me fall for you while planning to destroy me the whole time!"

"I know." Carson's hands clenched at his sides. "I know what I did. And there's nothing I can say that will make it right."

"Then why should I even be here?" Kinsley's eyes glistened with unshed tears. "Why did I come back? What the hell is wrong with me that even after everything, I still—"

She cut herself off, turning away.

Carson took a step toward her, then stopped. "Still what?"

Kinsley whirled back to face him, tears now streaming down her cheeks. "That I still love you, you bastard! I heard what you said in that warehouse. I heard you say you loved me, and god help me, I love you too!"

He staggered, catching himself on the edge of the couch. Inside his chest, disbelief went to war with a desperate, clawing hope.

"Kinsley—"

She crossed the distance between them in three quick steps and slapped him hard across the face.

Carson's head snapped to the side, the sting blooming across his cheek. When he looked back at her, her eyes were wild, her chest heaving.

And then she was kissing him.

Her mouth crashed against his, desperate and angry and hungry all at once. Carson froze for a heartbeat, then his arms came around her, pulling her against him as if he could meld their bodies together.

The kiss tasted of salt and brandy and forgiveness he didn't deserve. Kinsley's hands were in his hair, nails scraping his scalp, and he groaned into her mouth, walking her backward until her back hit the wall.

Her legs came up around his waist, and he caught her, supporting her weight easily as the kiss deepened, turned molten. His hands slid under her shirt, finding warm skin, and she gasped against his lips.

The elevator chimed.

Carson broke the kiss, confusion washing over him. No one had buzzed up. No one had access unless—

The doors slid open, and a man stepped out. Average height, nondescript features, unremarkable in every way except for the gun with a silencer in his hand.

Carson's brain processed the threat in milliseconds. He shoved Kinsley behind him just as the man raised the weapon.

The first shot caught Carson in the chest, the impact knocking him backward. He grabbed Kinsley as he fell, both of them tumbling over the back of the couch onto the floor.

White-hot pain exploded through him. It seared him. Kinsley screamed, her hands pressing against his chest where blood bloomed across his skin.

"Run," Carson gasped, hearing footsteps approaching the couch. "When I move, run for the elevator. Get out."

"Carson—"

"Please." He met her eyes, saw the terror there. "I can't lose you. Not again."

The footsteps drew closer. Carson gathered what strength he had left, pressed a hard, desperate kiss to Kinsley's mouth, then lunged up and over the couch.

He collided with the gunman, tackling him to the floor. Out of the corner of his eye, he saw Kinsley scramble up and run.

Relief washed through him, followed immediately by agony as the man beneath him drove a fist into his wound. Carson grunted, his vision swimming.

The man used Carson's moment of weakness to flip their positions, pinning Carson to the floor. Blow after blow rained down on Carson's face, each impact sending fresh waves of pain through his already damaged body.

"You don't even know who I am, do you?" the man snarled, pausing his assault.

Carson blinked through the blood dripping into his eyes. The face above him was unfamiliar, twisted with hatred.

"Michael Ashford," the man spat. "Richard Ashford's son."

Recognition dawned.

"You took everything from me," Michael continued, his hands wrapping around Carson's throat. "My father, my family's reputation, our money. Everything. You ruined my life."

Carson's airway constricted under the pressure. He clawed at Michael's hands, but his strength was fading, blood loss and pain making his movements sluggish.

"I'm sorry," Carson choked out. The words were barely audible, squeezed past Michael's grip.

Michael's hands tightened. "What?"

"I'm sorry," Carson repeated, forcing the words out. "What happened to your father... to you... I didn't plan his death."

"Bullshit!" Michael spat. "You destroyed him. You made it your mission."

"I exposed the truth," Carson gasped. "But I didn't... want him to die. Never wanted... you to suffer."

And it was true, Carson realized. Somewhere along the way— perhaps with Kinsley—he'd lost his taste for destruction. For revenge.

"Your father made his choices," Carson wheezed. "Just like I made mine. We were both... wrong."

Michael's face contorted. "Shut up! You don't get to apologize now!"

The pressure on Carson's throat increased. Blackness crept in at the edges of his vision. He thought of Kinsley, hoped she'd gotten to safety, hoped she knew how much he truly loved her.

As consciousness began to slip away, a loud crack split the air.

Michael jerked, a look of surprise crossing his face. He toppled forward, his weight crushing down on Carson's chest.

Carson gasped as air rushed back into his lungs. He shoved Michael's body off him, rolling to the side.

Kinsley stood there, Michael's gun trembling in her hands.

"Kinsley," Carson croaked, trying to push himself up.

The gun clattered to the floor as Kinsley dropped to her knees beside him.

"Oh god. I killed him. I...I didn't know what else to do. I c-called Jenna," she said, her voice shaking. "She's on her way. I was going to stay hidden, but then I heard—he was killing you—"

"It's okay," Carson murmured, reaching up to touch her face. "You saved me."

"I killed him. Oh god. And you..." Her hands pressed against his chest wound, trying to stem the bleeding. "You're hurt. Oh god, there's so much blood."

Carson tried to focus on her face, but his vision continued tunneling, even without Michael's hands on his throat. "Are you okay?"

A sob escaped her. "Am I okay? You got shot, you fucking idiot!"

"Worth it," he mumbled, his eyelids growing heavy. "To protect you."

"Don't you dare pass out on me, Carson," Kinsley demanded, tears streaming down her face. "Stay awake. Stay with me. Please."

Carson wanted to reassure her, to tell her again that he loved her, but darkness was pulling him under too quickly.

The last thing he heard was Kinsley's desperate voice. "I just forgave you. Don't you leave me now."

Darkness fell.

CHAPTER FIFTEEN

KINSLEY

KINSLEY SAT AT CARSON'S BEDSIDE FOR TWENTY EIGHT hours and sixteen minutes before he finally woke up after emergency surgery. It was another eight days before they finally let him leave, and she was pretty sure that was only because he bribed the hospital with a sizable donation.

Thankfully, Dr. Nikelson apparently did penthouse calls because Carson wasn't exactly back to his normal condition when he did get to go home.

Kinsley fluffed Carson's pillow for the third time in ten minutes, ignoring his amused expression.

"If you adjust that pillow one more time, I might have to fire you as my nurse," Carson said, his voice still a bit raspy but stronger than it had been in the hospital.

"As if you could find someone else willing to put up with your grumpy attitude." She straightened the already-straight blanket over his legs. "Dr. Nikelson said you need to stay hydrated. More water?"

Carson caught her wrist gently before she could reach for the glass on the nightstand. "Kinsley. Come here."

The softness in his voice made her pause. She'd been running on nervous energy since they'd arrived at his penthouse that morning, flitting around like a hummingbird, afraid to be still. Afraid to think too much about how close she'd come to losing him.

With a small sigh, she perched on the edge of the bed. Afternoon light bathed Carson's bedroom in gold, the city sprawling beyond his floor-to-ceiling windows.

"You haven't sat down all day," Carson said, his gray eyes studying her face. The bruises around his neck had faded to a yellowish green, but the bandage on his chest where the bullet had torn through remained stark white against his skin. "You're exhausted."

"I'm fine."

"Liar." His thumb traced circles on the inside of her wrist.

"I'm not the one who got shot, remember? You're the one who needs rest."

Carson's expression softened. "I'm sorry."

"For getting shot or for everything else?"

"Both. All of it." He shifted, wincing slightly as he moved. "But mostly for hurting you. For blaming you for something that wasn't your fault."

Kinsley looked down at their joined hands. They hadn't really talked about it, at least not properly. In the hospital, with doctors and nurses constantly coming and going, there hadn't been time or privacy. And she'd been too focused on his recovery to push.

Kinsley swallowed hard. "Paisley told me about Emma's illness."

"My sister talks too much."

"Your sister loves you." Kinsley hesitated. "She didn't even know what you'd done, and she still tried to put a good word in for you."

Carson sighed, leaning back against his pillows. "Pai is to good for her own good."

"That sounds redundant."

"She's a sweetheart."

Kinsley raised an eyebrow. "I thought I was the sweetheart."

He smiled, tugging her towards him by the wrist. "You're *my* sweetheart."

"I suppose I am." She reached out to brush a strand of hair from his forehead. "I still find it strange that somewhere along the way, while we were pretending, I actually fell for you."

Carson caught her hand and pressed it to his cheek. "It wasn't pretend. That's what terrified me. I started feeling things I never expected to feel again." His gaze held hers. "I love you, Kinsley. I think I've loved you for years."

"You mean when you were stalking me?"

"If that's what you want to call it," he said indignantly, but his lips curved into a smile.

"I'm pretty sure what you did is the definition of stalking."

'And yet?"

"And yet."

With only a moment's hesitation, Kinsley kicked off her shoes and carefully climbed onto the bed beside him, mindful of his injuries. Carson lifted his good arm, and she nestled against his uninjured side, her head resting on his chest where she could hear the steady rhythm of his heartbeat.

"Better?" she asked.

"Much." His fingers trailed through her curls. "Though I'm not sure Dr. Nikelson would approve of this particular recovery position."

"What Dr. Nikelson doesn't know won't hurt her."

They lay in comfortable silence for a while, the late afternoon light painting golden patterns across the bedspread.

"What happens now?" she asked eventually. "With your company, I mean. And the Ashford case."

"Benedict and the team are handling the fallout." Carson paused. "The police ruled Michael's death as self-defense. You saved my life, Kinsley."

She closed her eyes, trying not to remember the weight of the gun in her hands, the sound it made. "I didn't want to kill him."

"I know." Carson pressed a kiss to the top of her head. "But you did what you had to do. Just like when you held your own against those men in the warehouse."

"I was so angry when I saw you there," she admitted. "I thought, 'How dare he risk his life for me after everything he did?' But then when Lester had that gun to your head..." She shuddered at the memory.

"Not my finest moment," Carson said dryly. "Though I did get to make a dramatic love confession, so there's that."

Kinsley propped herself up on one elbow to look at him, careful not to put pressure on his injured side. "Was that really how you wanted to tell me? With a gun to your head in a dirty warehouse?"

"I had a much more elegant scenario planned." His expression grew serious. "But I meant every word, Kinsley. I thought I was going to die, and all I could think was that I'd never told you the truth about how I felt."

She traced the line of his jaw with her fingertip. "And what about my life? The contract I signed giving you control over my image?"

"Torn up. You're free to do whatever you want." He caught her hand and kissed her palm. "Though I hope whatever you choose includes me in some capacity."

"It will." Kinsley took a deep breath. "I'm thinking of starting a podcast," she said. "Something honest about mental health and social media. No filters, no perfectly curated image. Just... me. The real me."

Carson's eyes lit up. "The loud, opinionated version of you that I've caught glimpses of? I like her."

"You might be the only one."

"I doubt that very much." His thumb brushed across her bottom lip. "You're extraordinary when you're not trying to be what everyone else wants."

Warmth bloom in her chest.

Carson's hand slid to the back of her neck, his eyes darkening. "I've missed you," he murmured. "These past days in the hospital, having you so close but not being able to touch you properly..."

"Dr. Nikelson said you need to rest," she reminded him, even as she melted against him.

"I am resting. Very horizontally, as prescribed." His thumb traced the curve of her ear, sending shivers down her spine. "Besides, I think I've earned at least a kiss after taking a bullet."

"You're going to milk that for all it's worth, aren't you?"

"Absolutely." His smile was unrepentant. "Is it working?"

Instead of answering, Kinsley closed the distance between them. The kiss was gentle at first, mindful of his injuries, but quickly deepened as weeks of fear and longing poured out between them. Carson's hand tangled in her hair, holding her close as though afraid she might disappear.

When they finally broke apart, both slightly breathless, Kinsley rested her forehead against his. "I should probably let you rest for real."

"Stay," Carson whispered. "Please."

The vulnerability in that single word had exactly the effect he seemed to be looking for. Carson grinned as she sighed. Kinsley settled back against him, her head finding its place on his chest, his heartbeat steady beneath her ear.

"I'm not going anywhere," she promised.

Outside, the sun began to set, painting the Manhattan skyline in shades of pink and gold. Carson's breathing gradually evened out as he drifted to sleep, his arm still wrapped securely around her.

As the last rays of sunlight faded from the room, Kinsley pressed a gentle kiss to Carson's chest, right over his heart. "I love you," she whispered to his sleeping form.

In his sleep, Carson's arm tightened around her. Kinsley smiled and closed her eyes, letting herself be held.

EPILOGUE
2 YEARS LATER - KINSLEY

KINSLEY ELLIS STEPPED OUT OF THE ELEVATOR ONTO THE top floor of the Crest Strategies building. The receptionist smiled at her, waving her through. She was a regular there now, and not just because she was engaged to the CEO. Over the past two years, she'd worked closely with the team on various projects, using her podcasting platform to advocate for mental health awareness and against the cancel culture that very nearly ruined her.

She balanced the takeout bags in one hand as she pushed open the heavy door leading to Carson's office. He was on the phone, his back to her, gazing out at the sprawling Manhattan skyline. His charcoal suit hugged his frame perfectly.

"...understand your concerns, sir," Carson was saying in a strong, reassuring voice. "I assure you, we have the best team in the business. We'll have your company's image rebuilt in no time."

Kinsley set the bags down on the sleek black desk, the aroma of gourmet Italian filling the room. Carson turned, his eyes lighting up when he saw her. He held up a finger, signaling he'd be just a moment.

"Yes, I understand," he said into the phone, his gaze never leaving Kinsley. "We'll discuss this further in our meeting next week. Enjoy your weekend. Yes, of course. Goodbye."

He hung up, tossing the phone onto the desk with a clatter. "Sweetheart," he greeted. "You're a sight for sore eyes."

She smiled, walking around the desk to meet him. "Rough morning?"

"Just the usual headaches," he said, pulling her into his arms. He kissed her.

Kinsley melted into him, her hands gripping his lapels. When they finally broke apart, she was breathless. "I thought you might need a break," she said, gesturing to the takeout bags. "And some fuel."

Carson raised an eyebrow. "Is that all you brought me?" he asked, his voice a low rumble.

She laughed, swatting his chest. "Behave. We have a wedding to plan, remember?"

"How could I forget?" he murmured, releasing her to dig into the takeout bags. "You've been sending me links to beachside venues nonstop."

Kinsley sat down in one of the plush leather chairs across from the desk, watching as Carson unpacked the food. "You're the one who suggested a destination wedding," she reminded him.

"I did, didn't I?" He grinned, handing her a plate of pasta. "Well, I can't wait to see you in a bikini for a week straight."

She rolled her eyes, even as heat pooled in her belly. "Is that the only reason you wanted a beach wedding?"

"Of course not," he said, sitting down next to her. "I also can't wait to see you *out* of a bikini."

Kinsley laughed, shaking her head.

"How was your day," he said, taking a bite of his pasta.

"Good," she said, glancing down at her engagement ring, a stunning three-carat diamond set in a platinum band. It was simple, elegant, and perfect. "Pai and I have been working on that nonprofit that we're hoping will connect those struggling with depression with the resources they need, but Ben pulled her away."

"I don't want to know." Carson wrinkled his nose.

"I doubted you would." Kinsley stirred the pasta sauce around the noodles. They continued to chat about the day as they ate. Just like every time the discussion of the wedding came up, Kinsley's heart fluttered faster.

"So have you given any more thought to the honeymoon?" Kinsley asked, twirling her pasta around her fork.

Carson nodded, a mischievous glint in his eye. "I have a few ideas," he said. "But I'm not telling you until it's all planned out."

"Why not?" she pouted.

He leaned in, his voice lowering. "Because, I like to keep you on your toes. And besides," he added, moving around his desk and leaning down over her. His hand slid up her thigh, "I enjoy seeing that look of surprise on your face."

Kinsley's breath hitched as his hand inched higher, her skin tingling beneath his touch. "Carson," she warned, her voice barely above a whisper. "I didn't lock the door."

"And?" he challenged, his fingers tracing the lace edge of her panties. "I own the building, sweetheart. I can do whatever I want."

She bit her lip, a shiver running down her spine.

"What do you want, Kinsley?" he murmured, his fingers stilling.

She looked into his eyes, seeing the darkness that still lingered there. His darkness likely matched her own. She knew what he needed, what they both needed.

"I want you. Always," she said, her voice steady. "Take control."

A slow smile spread across Carson's face, and he stood, offering her his hand. "Come," he said, leading her to the floor-to-ceiling windows that overlooked the city.

He positioned her in front of him, her back to his chest, his hands gripping her hips. His erection pressed against her, and she leaned back, grinding against him. He groaned, his fingers digging into her flesh.

"You are my drug," he growled. "I need you injected straight into my veins. Every day. All the time."

She smirked, looking at him over her shoulder. "Good."

Kinsley's breath fogged up the glass as Carson's hands slid down her thighs, bunching up her skirt. His fingers traced the edge of her panties before slipping beneath the lace. She moaned, her head falling back onto his shoulder as he began to stroke her, his touch igniting a fire.

"Carson," she whispered, her voice barely audible over the hum of the city below. His fingers moved, circling and teasing, pushing her closer and closer to the edge.

She reached up, her hand cupping the back of his neck, pulling him down for a kiss. Their tongues clashed, the taste of him intoxicating. She moaned into his mouth, her hips grinding against his hand, seeking more friction. He growled in response, his fingers moving faster, pushing her higher.

But just as she was about to tumble over the edge, he stopped. Carson spun her around, his hands gripping her waist as he lifted her onto the desk. Papers scattered, falling to the floor in a flutter of white.

"Take me," she begged, her voice breathy. She spread her legs, inviting him in, her heels hooking around his thighs.

He stood between her knees, his hands gripping her thighs. "That's what I plan on doing, sweetheart."

She leaned back, her hands braced on the desk, her chest heaving.

He leaned down, his hands sliding up her thighs, his fingers hooking onto her panties. He tugged, the lace tearing beneath his touch. She giggled, her hips lifting off the desk as he tossed the scrap of fabric aside.

Carson undid his belt, the leather sliding through the loops with a hiss. His pants hit the floor, followed by his boxers. He stood before her, half naked with his cock hard and ready. She reached for him, her fingers wrapping around his length, stroking him.

He grabbed her wrist, pulling her hand away. "You said take control. I'm in control," he growled. He pushed her further onto the desk, her legs dangling over the edge. Carson's fingers dug into her flesh as he spread her wide.

Kinsley propped herself higher on her elbows, her gaze locked onto his as he guided himself to her entrance.

With one swift thrust, he was inside her. She cried out, her back arching off the desk. He stilled, his breath coming in ragged gasps, his eyes locked onto hers.

"You always feel so good," he groaned, his voice strained. "So fucking good."

She smiled, her hands reaching up to cup his face. "So do you," she said, her voice soft, her eyes shining with love. "Now fuck me like you mean it, Carson."

He pulled out, searched her eyes for less than a moment, before he surged forward.

Kinsley cried out, her nails digging into his skin. He leaned over her, his hands braced on either side of her head, caging her in. Pinned beneath him, her chest heaved as he began to move.

His hips snapped forward, his cock thrusting deep. Her walls clenched around him, the friction igniting a furnace in her belly. She loved the burn. He groaned, his eyes falling shut as he withdrew before snapping his hips forward again. A sharp slap echoed through the room as his hand connected with her ass.

"Fuck!" she cried out, her head falling back as he thrust into her again.

"Look at me," he ordered, his voice harsh.

She opened her eyes, meeting his intense gaze. His thumb stroked her jaw, his fingers tangling in her hair, tilting her head back to expose her neck. Every inch of her lay on display for his pleasure.

Another slap echoed, the sting radiating across her thigh. She yelped and let out a low chuckle, her hips bucking to meet his. He thrust into her, his pace frantic, his eyes never leaving hers.

"You drive me crazy," he growled, his thumb stroking her bottom lip. "From the moment I saw you, I couldn't get you out of my head."

"Carson," she moaned, her walls clenching around him, her body winding tighter and tighter.

He leaned down, his lips brushing hers. "You are mine," he demanded, his breath warm against her mouth. "Mine. My brave, strong, woman."

He pulled back, his eyes searching hers as he snapped his hips forward. "And so fucking beautiful."

"Carson, please," she begged, her body on edge, hovering just out of reach.

He chuckled. "Please what? Explicit requests, sweetheart."

"I want you," she panted. "Harder."

A dark smile curved his lips, and he withdrew before thrusting his hips forward, his cock sinking deep. His hand curled around her throat, his thumb stroking her jaw. "Like this?"

"Yes," she moaned, her head falling back, baring her neck.

He pistoned his hips, his hand tightening around her throat. "Mine," he growled, his breath fanning her chest, making her nipples peak. "Always mine."

Her vision blurred, the room spinning as he choked her. She loved it, the surrender, the loss of control. He owned her, body and soul, and she reveled in it.

His thumb stroked her cheek as his other hand slid down her body, his fingers finding her clit. He rubbed slow circles as he thrust into her, his pace relentless. She felt stretched, filled, the pleasure coiling like a spring ready to send her flying over the edge.

"Come for me," he ordered, his voice harsh.

His fingers circled faster, his hips snapping forward. She cried out, her body snapping taut, pleasure exploding through her. She tightened around him, milking his cock as he thrust into her, his own release washing over him with her name on his tongue.

"Kinsley, fuck..."

He rode out her waves, his cock emptying inside her as he buried his face in her neck, his breath warm against her skin. "I love you," he whispered.

She smiled, her hands stroking his back, feeling the ridges of his scar tissue beneath her fingertips. "I love you too," she whispered back.

He nipped her neck, his hands gently caressing her throat before trailing down her body. "Marry me," he murmured against her skin. "Make me the happiest man alive, Kinsley Ellis."

She giggled, stroking her fingers through his hair. "I'm pretty sure I already agreed to that."

"I want to hear you say it again," Carson murmured, his thumb tracing her jawline. "Say you'll be mine forever."

Kinsley gazed up at him, at the vulnerability in his steel-gray eyes that only she got to see. Two years ago, she would never have imagined being here—engaged to the man who had once plotted her destruction, now planning their future together.

"I'll marry you, Carson Crest," she whispered, her fingers threading through his hair. "I am yours forever."

He kissed her then, soft and sweet, so different from the frantic passion of moments before. When he pulled away, his eyes sparkled with a contentment that still surprised her sometimes.

"We should probably clean up before your next meeting," she said, glancing at the scattered papers on the floor.

Carson chuckled, helping her sit up. "I doubt the guys would appreciate seeing my dick as much as you."

Kinsley threw her head back and laughed.

As they straightened their clothes, Kinsley's phone chimed with a text. She fished it from her purse, reading the message from Paisley.

"Pai wants to know if we're still on for dinner tonight," she said. "Apparently Ben has something he wants to tell us."

Carson rolled his eyes. "If my best friend is planning to propose to my sister over dinner, I'm walking out."

"You will not," Kinsley laughed, fixing her hair in the reflection of the window. "You'll sit there and be happy for them, just like they were happy for us."

"Fine," he grumbled, but she caught the small smile tugging at his lips. "But I'm not pretending to be surprised. Benedict's been carrying that ring around for months."

Kinsley shook her head, remembering how Benedict had nervously shown her the ring before he'd bought it, asking if Paisley would like it. The man could barely keep his hands from shaking when talking about proposing to the woman he loved.

"Some things are worth the wait," she said softly.

Carson came up behind her, wrapping his arms around her waist and resting his chin on her shoulder. Their reflection stared back at them from the window. Her in her floral dress, him in his tailored suit, both of them slightly disheveled but glowing.

She reached up and touched his face, grinning at his reflection.

He leaned into her, turning to kiss her palm. The gesture was so tender it made her heart ache.

A knock at the door interrupted them. Carson sighed, stepping back as his assistant poked her head in.

"Mr. Crest, your three o'clock is here."

"Thank you. I'll be right out."

When the door closed, Kinsley gathered the takeout containers. "I should go. I have a podcast to record this afternoon."

Carson nodded, helping her clean up. "Then I'll see you when I get home?"

"Absolutely." She reached up on tiptoes to kiss him goodbye. "I love you."

"Love you more, sweetheart," he murmured against her lips.

READ THE FIRST CHAPTER IN THE
NEXT NOVELLA IN THE BILLIONAIRES
OF CREST STRATEGIES SERIES

A DARK BILLIONAIRE ROMANCE NOVELLA

TATTERED
Secrets

ELORA RAE

CHAPTER 1
BENEDICT

No amount of money could buy the heart of Paisley Crest, and that knowledge killed Benedict Astor as he watched his best friend's sister steal the hearts of every man and woman in the ballroom.

Benedict positioned himself where he always did—in the shadows, where he could see everything without being seen. The dim corner of the ballroom afforded him the perfect vantage point to observe the charity gala's attendees, but his gaze tracked only one person.

Paisley.

She moved through the crowd in a deep blue silk dress that clung to curves he'd memorized from years of watching from afar. The fabric caught the light when she turned, creating shadows and highlights across her body that he could have mapped with his eyes closed. Her dark curls were pinned up, exposing the nape of her neck. He would've paid anything to be able to press his lips there. To feel her soft skin. Hear her moan against him.

This was his purgatory. Watching. Wanting. Never having.

God, Carson would kill Benedict if he knew that his best friend and business partner was in love with his baby sister.

Benedict adjusted his collar. It was too hot in there. It certainly had nothing to do with the effect Paisley had on him. The damn tie was just too tight. And his trousers. They were feeling too tight too when just a little while ago, before a certain distraction arrived, his suit had been impeccable, his posture perfect, his expression neutral. Only his gaze revealed the truth as it followed her.

He was her protector. At least, that's what he told himself to justify the way he kept track of her.

"You look like you're planning a hit," Carson said, appearing at Benedict's side with two whiskeys. He handed one to Benedict. "Stop scowling. It's a party."

Benedict accepted the drink without shifting his gaze. "I don't have to be the face of the company. That's your job." He poked Carson in the chest.

"So you're saying I can't pay you to switch places with me?" Carson teased.

"There is not enough money in the world. Besides," Benedict took a slow sip of whiskey, letting it burn down his throat. "I have everything I want."

Except Paisley.

Carson snorted. "I suppose that's true." He clapped Benedict's shoulder. "I guess I should go mingle. I'll send you a text if I need rescuing."

"I'll make sure to put my phone on do not disturb."

Benedict smirked, watching as Carson flipped him off and rejoined the party. His best friend commanded attention in a way Benedict never could. Carson's easy confidence was why he was the face of their reputation management business. Not Benedict, and certainly not the other three men, though James probably would do well. Better than Tanner or Penn.

Across the room, Paisley laughed at something someone said, the sound carrying over the ambient noise. Benedict tensed, finding her instantly.

He took another sip of whiskey, watching as a man approached Paisley, leaning in too close. Bastard. Benedict's fingers tightened around the glass, knuckles whitening. The stranger's hand settled on the small of her back, and Benedict's jaw clenched hard enough to hurt.

Twelve years. He'd been in this private hell for twelve years.

He'd met her at Carson's birthday celebration. Benedict had been twenty-one himself, fresh out of college and working his way through business school, determined to build something that would matter.

Carson had made the introduction. Paisley had been a beautiful young woman of eighteen with wild curls and freckles scattered across her nose. She'd worn a simple sundress, nothing fancy. And yet Benedict had choked on his drink at the sight of her.

When he'd introduced himself, extending his hand, she'd ignored it completely, instead throwing her arms around him and telling him that any friend of Carson's was family to her.

The hug had lasted seconds. Maybe less. But in that moment, with her pressed against him and the scent of her shampoo filling his lungs, Benedict had known with absolute certainty that Paisley Crest would ruin him.

That certainty had only grown stronger over the years.

Benedict watched as Paisley extricated herself from the man's grasp with a smile. She had a gift for letting people down without making them feel rejected. It was part of what made her so dangerous to him. She held genuine kindness in those brown eyes, and she actually cared about everyone's feelings.

Everyone except his, because she had no idea how he felt.

His phone vibrated in his pocket. A text from one of the people who worked under him.

> Surveillance is complete for the Hamilton case.
> Files uploaded to secure server.

Benedict replied with a simple acknowledgment. Crest Strategies never stopped working, even during their own charity events. Carson might be the face, but Benedict was the spine, the one who kept everything aligned, who anticipated problems before they materialized.

Which was why he noticed immediately when Paisley's behavior shifted.

She'd been in the middle of a conversation with the nonprofit director when her phone lit up. Her expression changed. Though she still smiled, her eyes tightened and her lips parted. Excusing herself, she turned and moved toward the exit.

Benedict set his glass down. Something was wrong.

He tracked her movement through the crowd, maintaining his distance but never losing sight of her. She slipped through the ballroom doors, bypassing the coat check and heading for the private elevator—the one that led to the Crest Strategies offices upstairs.

Benedict waited thirty seconds before following. The elevator was already gone when he reached it, the digital display showing it had stopped at the office suite.

He pressed the call button, keeping his face neutral despite the confusion churning inside him. Why would Paisley go to their offices during the gala? The entire staff was downstairs. The offices would be empty.

When the elevator arrived, he stepped inside and pressed the button, then leaned against the wall as the doors closed. His mind cataloged possibilities: perhaps she needed something from Carson's office? Maybe she'd forgotten an item earlier in the day when she'd stopped by to have lunch with her brother?

None of the explanations felt right.

The elevator doors opened silently onto the darkened reception area. The motion sensors detected his presence, illuminating the space with soft light. Benedict moved through the familiar halls, listening for any sound that might reveal Paisley's location.

The main workspace was empty. So was the conference room. He moved down the hallway toward the executive offices, pausing outside each door to listen before continuing.

When he reached Carson's office at the end of the hall, the sound of pages moving slipped through the crack in the door inside. It was ajar, a sliver of light spilling into the corridor. Benedict approached, moving as quietly as he could. He positioned himself to see through the narrow opening without being seen.

Paisley stood at Carson's desk, rifling through papers. She chewed on the edge of her thumb as she scanned the lines of text. Her brow furrowed. She flipped to the next. And the next.

She was searching for something specific.

Benedict watched as she opened a drawer, removed a file, and began photographing its contents with her phone. His blood ran cold. This wasn't innocent. This was... infiltration.

He pushed the door open. "Pai?"

She jumped, dropping her phone with a clatter. When she turned to face him, her eyes were wide. A second later, though, determination replaced the surprise.

"Ben." His name came out breathless. She pressed a hand to her chest. "You scared me."

"What are you doing in here?" He kept his voice even.

"I just needed to grab something from Carson's office." A lie. She'd lied to his face. Benedict had studied her expressions, cataloged her tells. The slight flutter of her eyelashes. The way she chewed the inside of her cheek or the edge of her thumb.

"Try again." He stepped into the office, closing the door behind him. "This time with the truth."

Paisley's shoulders slumped. She bent to retrieve her phone, tucking it into her clutch. "It's not what it looks like."

"It looks like you're going through your brother's confidential files and photographing them." Benedict moved closer, his footsteps silent on the plush carpet. "Please tell me there's an explanation that doesn't involve corporate espionage."

"Corporate espionage?" She laughed, but it sounded hollow. "Don't be dramatic."

"Then what is it?" He was close enough now to smell her perfume; something floral with undertones of vanilla. Close enough to see the pulse jumping in her throat.

"I can't tell you." She met his gaze directly, chin lifted in defiance. "But I need you to trust me."

"Trust works both ways." He gestured to the open file on the desk. "This doesn't look like trust."

She took a step toward him, and Benedict fought the urge to

retreat. It didn't matter that she barely came up to his chest. Paisley Crest could be just as intimidating as her brother when she wanted to be. It also didn't help that being this close to her was dangerous. She made it harder to think clearly, to remember why he needed to keep his distance.

"There are things about Crest Strategies that you don't know," she said quietly. "Things Carson is hiding."

Benedict's expression remained impassive, but his mind raced. "Carson and I built this company together. There's nothing about it I don't know."

"Are you sure about that?" Her gaze searched his face. "The Jennings account. Have you looked into it personally?"

"I know what it is."

"It's a high-profile divorce case you all took about five months ago."

"I'm aware." He shrugged, sliding his hands into his pockets. "I was in charge of the surveillance. But why do you care about it?"

"The wife." Paisley's voice dropped to a whisper. "She disappeared two days ago."

"People disappear all the time during contentious divorces." His response was automatic. "They go to friends, family, hotels under assumed names."

"Police found her car abandoned on the side of the road. Blood in the trunk."

A chill ran down Benedict's spine. "And you think this has something to do with us? Really? Come on, Pai." He frowned at her. "We're the good guys here."

Well, most of the time.

There had been occasions where Crest Strategies had used its resources to put well-deserving criminals into the metaphorical ground. But he knew for a fact that the Jennings case was not one of them. The wife had been their client. Their job was to protect her and help her win her case against her abusive husband.

Benedict was about to point this out when Paisley continued.

"I think it has something to do with Tanner." Paisley held up her phone, showing him a series of text messages. "He's been in contact with Jenning's private security team. Secret meetings, off the books."

Benedict's mind processed the information, even as he shook his head. If what she was saying was true, it meant someone at Crest Strategies—someone he trusted—was operating outside their ethical boundaries. Outside the law. Sure, Tanner was the go-to clean-up guy, but they reserved that for messier cases. Mrs. Jennings was an easy client.

"Tanner wouldn't do that." Benedict straightened, rolling his shoulders back. At least, he thought, not without Carson's instructions.

"Why are you investigating this?" he asked. "Why not go to the police?"

"With what evidence? Text messages that could be about anything?" She shook her head. "I needed proof before I brought this to Carson. Or to you."

"You think I'm involved." It wasn't a question.

"I think you see the best in your friends." Her expression softened. "Even when evidence suggests otherwise."

"You just said you don't have evidence."

"Well, that's what I was looking for." She gestured towards the desk.

Benedict closed his eyes briefly, forcing himself to think logically rather than emotionally. He highly doubted reserved and controlled Tanner had gone rogue. For Tanner to make things or people disappear, all five Crest Strategies men had to agree, and they hadn't even discussed it. But if Paisley was right, though he still doubted she was, and his friend was involved in something illegal, they needed to handle it internally before it destroyed everything they'd built.

"Alright," he said, sighing. "Show me what you've found." He moved to the desk, standing close enough that their shoulders almost touched.

Paisley hesitated, then pulled out her phone again. "These are texts between Tanner and Mr. Jennings from last week." She scrolled through screenshots. "And these are surveillance photos my contact took of them meeting at a warehouse in the industrial district."

Benedict studied the images. "Your contact?" His mind calculated potential damage and containment strategies. "Who else knows about this?"

"Just me." She bit the side of her thumbnail.

"And this contact." He shook his head. "Who is it, Pai? Who sent you these?"

"I...I can't tell you." She put her phone away and took a step back. "Sorry, but I couldn't risk going to Carson until I was certain. He and Tanner are too close."

"And you thought I'd be more objective?" He raised an eyebrow.

"Well, you didn't give me much of a choice, barreling in here." She dropped his gaze. "But I did think you'd be more rational." Her eyes met his. "You almost always are."

The compliment shouldn't have affected him, but it did. Even now, with everything she'd implied about his friend, a treacherous warmth spread through his chest.

"What are you going to do now that you know?" She asked as she wrapped her arms around herself. "Are you going to tell Carson about all of this?"

"I..." Benedict ran a hand through his sandy blonde hair and shook his head. "I don't know."

Benedict's mind raced through calculations and consequences. The possibility that Tanner was operating outside their established protocols felt like a crack in the foundation of everything he'd built with Carson. It also was highly unlikely. But there was something else clouding his judgment. Or rather, someone. The woman standing before him, her brown eyes wide with concern, waiting for his answer.

"I really should tell Carson," he said, rubbing the back of his neck. "But..."

"But what?" Paisley stepped closer, her perfume invading his senses again.

"But I need to verify your information first." His voice remained steady despite the chaos in his mind. "If I go to Carson with accusations against Tanner without concrete evidence, it could fracture everything."

"So you'll help me?" Hope brightened her expression.

Benedict closed his eyes briefly. This was dangerous territory. Getting involved in Paisley's investigation meant spending time with her. Alone. It meant trusting her judgment. It meant keeping secrets from Carson.

It meant being near her. Constantly.

Maybe that's what pushed him over the edge.

"Yes," he finally said, opening his eyes to find her watching him intently. "I'll help you. But we do this my way. That means no more sneaking around, especially in Carson's office. This room is off limits when he's not here, even for me. God only knows what he'd do if he found out we were in here."

Relief softened her features. "Thank you, Benny."

The nickname sent an electric current through him that gathered at the base of his spine.

"Don't thank me yet." He moved to Carson's desk, carefully returning the files to their original positions. "This could be nothing. Or it could be something that destroys Crest Strategies. And then we're all screwed."

"Or saves it," she countered, helping him reorganize the desk.

Their hands brushed as they both reached for the same folder. Benedict froze, shocks shooting up his arm from that simple contact. Paisley paused too, her gaze darting to his face before quickly looking away.

"Sorry," she murmured, withdrawing her hand.

Benedict cleared his throat. "We should get back to the event before someone notices we're both missing."

"Right." She nodded, but made no move to leave. Instead, she chewed her bottom lip. "Ben, there's something else, but I need you to promise not to freak out."

"Freak out?" He turned to face her fully. "Why would I freak out?"

"It's just...I've felt for a while that someone's been... watching me." Her voice dropped to barely above a whisper. "Following me, maybe. I thought I was being paranoid, but I noticed the same car outside my building and my office, and... I don't know. It feels off. And I thought maybe, with you being in charge of surveillance and all, you might be willing to look into it."

Benedict froze. He'd been monitoring her for years, for her protection, he told himself, but he'd been meticulous, invisible. If she'd sensed surveillance, it wasn't his.

Which meant someone else was watching Paisley.

"When did this start?" His voice came out sharper than intended.

"A few months ago. Just... feelings at first. Then I noticed the car multiple nights in a row."

Benedict's protective instincts surged forward, drowning out his professional detachment. "Description?"

"Dark sedan. Tinted windows. I couldn't see the driver."

His mind was already mapping security protocols, calculating risks. "You should stay at Carson's until we figure this out."

"Hell no." She shook her head. "I'm not running scared. It might be nothing. And I'm not telling Carson until we know what's happening."

Their gazes locked in a silent battle. Benedict recognized the stubborn set of her jaw. It was the same expression Carson wore when his mind was made up.

"Fine then, you'll stay with me," he said before he could stop himself.

Paisley's eyes widened. "What?"

"My penthouse has state-of-the-art security. No one gets in without my knowledge. It's the logical solution."

A slow blush crept across her cheeks. "You want me to move in with you?"

"Temporarily," he clarified, ignoring how his heart raced at the thought. "For your protection."

"Carson will be pissed."

"Why? I'd like to think he'd appreciate me looking after his little sister."

Her face dropped, and she gave a small nod. "Right. His little sister." The small chuckle she gave lacked any heart. "I suppose all five of you see me that way."

He wanted to tell her he didn't. Instead, he bit his tongue hard enough to draw blood.

"Okay," she finally said. "When do I move in?"

"Tonight." His voice dropped lower. "After the event."

"Tonight then," she repeated.

READ THE REST OF BENEDICT AND PAISLEY'S STORY IN THE NEXT BILLIONAIRES OF CREST STRATEGIES NOVELLA:

TATTERED Secrets

MAKE SURE TO CHECK OUT
ALL FIVE BOOKS IN THE
BILLIONAIRES OF CREST STRATEGIES SERIES

ACKNOWLEDGMENTS

Holy hell.

I actually published a book. If you're reading this, that means *Ruined Lies* is officially out in the wild, probably wreaking havoc and making people fall in love with the wrong man for all the right reasons. I always said I wanted to write something dark and a bit unhinged. Welp. Here we are.

First, I want to thank my parents, who don't really understand why their daughter writes about obsessive billionaires with morally questionable hobbies but supported me anyway. And to my brother, who absolutely did *not* read this book (I don't blame you), but still told his friends, "My sister's an author now," with enough pride to make me cry a little. Love you Cody.

Next, a huge shoutout to my beta readers who rode the rollercoaster with me from chapter one to "oh no he did not." Thank you to Dani R., whose live reactions gave me life (and ego boosts). To Mariah S., who screamed at all the right parts and offered spicy edits without judgment. To Rachel H., who said "he's not toxic enough" and challenged me to dig deeper into my black soul. And to Grace L., for being the friend who always said, "Finish the damn book." Well, I did.

This is my debut, and to be honest, I didn't think I'd ever be brave enough to share it. But there's something magical about writing the kind of romance I've always devoured. The twisted, obsessive, messy kind. It's nice to know there are other people out there who love it too (I'm looking at you BookTok girlies).

To every reader who picked this book up: thank you for letting me ruin you just a little. I promise this is only the beginning.

Stay obsessed,

Elora Rae

ABOUT THE AUTHOR

Elora Rae is a longtime lover of dark romance, drawn to stories about morally grey men, obsessive love, and twisted secrets. When she's not writing, Elora is probably re-reading her favorite villain origin love stories or plotting the next emotionally delicious downfall. *Ruined Lies* is just the beginning.

www.ingramcontent.com/pod-product-compliance
Lightning Source LLC
Chambersburg PA
CBHW021159130626
46554CB00005B/1886